The Earl's Secret Bargain

Marriage by Deceit Series, Volume 1

Ruth Ann Nordin

Published by Ruth Ann Nordin, 2023.

The Earl's Secret Bargain
Published by Ruth Ann Nordin

Cover Photo images Period Images. http://www.periodimages.com/welcome-to-periodimagescom. All rights reserved – used with permission.
Cover Photo images Dreamstime. www.dreamstime.com. All rights reserved – used with permission.
Cover created by Stephannie Beman. www.stephanniebeman.com

Dedication: To Tina Phelps Grace who's been very sweet to me. Thank you!

Chapter One

June 1815

"I can get any lady I want."

Toby York, the Earl of Davenport, told himself not to oblige the boasting gentleman by giving him the attention he was obviously calling for. Nothing good would come of it. Let someone else fall in to whatever trap he'd snare them into. And yet... He found himself looking up from his cards in time to see Lord Pennella sit in a chair near a large window. With a smirk, Pennella placed his hands behind his head and carefully examined the other gentlemen who were at White's—a silent challenge in his eyes.

Toby glanced at Orlando Emmett, the Earl of Reddington, who sat across from him. Orlando made a show of rolling his eyes, and Toby grinned at his friend's silent joke.

"Is something amusing in my statement, Davenport?" Pennella called out.

Surprised that Pennella should single him out in a room full of ten gentlemen, Toby reluctantly looked in his direction. "No, nothing's amusing about you." When the gentlemen chuckled, he realized his blunder and cleared his throat. His face warm, he quickly added, "I meant, there was nothing amusing about what you said."

Pennella shifted in his chair and leaned forward, his voice loud enough to catch everyone's attention. "I assure you that I make no idle boast. I am one of the handsomest and wealthiest bachelors in London. I can get any lady I want, and I can get her with the snap of my fingers." As if he felt he needed to emphasize his point, he snapped his fingers.

Toby resisted the urge to roll his eyes. Braggart. Pennella was nothing but a braggart. And the problem was, everyone at White's was too afraid to stand up to him. Even Orlando gave a slight shake of his head to warn Toby not to engage the gentleman further. His friend was right. Toby would be wise to heed his advice.

"I have no doubt that you can get any lady you desire," Toby finally told Pennella.

Turning his attention back to the cards, he hoped that would be the end of it, but Pennella rose to his feet and walked over to him in slow, purposeful steps. Though Toby didn't look up from his cards immediately, he could feel the weight of everyone's stares in the room. He clenched his jaw in irritation. Pennella wanted a confrontation. He was looking for a fight, and it didn't matter who it was. This wasn't the first time Toby had seen it, but it was the first time he was the target.

Releasing his breath, he looked up from his cards at Pennella who stood over him. "What do you want with me? I already conceded to your claim."

"You don't believe me. You merely say you believe me to save your reputation in front of the others."

"Save my reputation?"

"Certainly. You suspected I was going to present an interesting wager and knew you'd lose. I understand you wish to be spared the humiliation of losing but—"

"Wait a minute." Toby straightened in his chair and set the cards down. "You never said—or implied—anything about a wager."

His eyebrows rose. "I didn't?"

Toby blinked. What was he up to?

"I can't say I'm surprised. How many hands have you lost at the gambling tables?"

"I'm not playing for money," he argued and gestured to Orlando. "This is a friendly game and nothing more."

"That hasn't always been true, has it? You have played for money in the past. I believe Edon has taken a good amount from you."

"Edon wins every game he plays. No one has ever beaten him."

"And that's not from lack of trying to lose," Lord Edon muttered, causing a round of laughter from everyone but Toby and Pennella.

After a tense moment passed between the two gentlemen, Toby decided he'd had enough. Everyone bowed to Pennella and gave him whatever he wanted. It was time someone stood up to him. Toby rose to his feet, pulling himself to his full height, which was just a half-inch shorter than Pennella. But he was able to see him eye to eye and that's what mattered.

"Why don't you just come out and tell me what you want?" Toby finally demanded.

"So you do wish for a challenge after all? I suppose it's only fitting if you want to save your pride."

With a roll of his eyes, he said, "Get on with it. You obviously came to White's planning to snare someone into a trap. So get on with it already."

Pennella stiffened.

Toby found minor satisfaction in catching him off guard. No doubt, he hadn't expected Toby to call him out on trying to wiggle someone into a wager they didn't want. He had wanted to word things in a way so that Toby seemed like the instigator. Since Toby hadn't played along, he remained silent for a long moment, probably trying to figure out the safest reply he could make.

"Fine," he finally replied, glancing at the other gentlemen before turning his gaze back to him. "I suggest a wager."

When he didn't say anything else, Toby shrugged. "I gathered that much. Is this wager going to involve money?"

The corner of his mouth twitched. "Would it be an interesting wager if there wasn't money involved?"

"Fine, then state your terms."

"Our estates."

It took Toby a moment to make sure he understood him right, and the only reason he realized he did was because Orlando's jaw practically dropped all the way to the floor. "You can't be serious."

"So you are afraid you'll lose."

"An estate is absurd. No gentleman in his right mind would bet something so outrageous."

"The higher the stakes, the more interesting the bet. But that's not the best part."

"Oh? You have plans to wager our mothers, too?"

The retort rewarded Toby with a few chuckles, but the tension in the room was still thick.

"My mother is no longer alive, so consider yours safe," Pennella replied.

So was Toby's, but he kept silent.

"The focus of our little wager will be the hand of a lady. Whichever one of us gets a certain lady to accept our marriage proposal gets the other's estate."

"You can't bet on a lady," Lord Roderick intervened.

"Why not?" Pennella asked.

"Because it's immoral to bet on a human being. Estates are one thing, but a person—"

"You are ever so dull, Roderick, but I don't believe this has anything to do with you." Pennella turned his attention back to Toby. "We will pick one lady. The one she chooses wins."

Toby gritted his teeth and thought over the ramifications of the bet. If he refused, he'd never live it down. As much as he hated to admit it, his pride was one of the few things he had left. And besides, it wasn't like he had much left to his estate after his father gambled so much money away, but only Orlando—his most trusted friend—knew his shame. So what did he have to lose?

Pennella wouldn't really win anything, and that would serve him right. All Toby had to do was pick a lady who'd never pick Pennella. Then when she chose him, he wouldn't hold her to a marriage with him. That way, the lady wouldn't be a pawn in this whole thing. At least not in the end. Considering he was backed into a corner, it was the best he could do.

"I'll agree to your terms," Toby began, "on one condition."

Pennella's lips twitched. "And what would that be?"

"I get to select the lady."

"Now, that's hardly fair, is it? For all I know, you could pick someone you already know."

"I won't, but you'll have to take my word for it." When Pennella frowned, he shrugged. "Unless you're that worried you'll lose. In that case, I'll let you gracefully bow out of the wager before you embarrass yourself."

"No," he snapped then cleared his throat and adjusted his cravat. "I made no idle boast. I can have any lady."

"Fine. Then you have nothing to worry about if I choose her."

After a long moment, he sighed. "Very well, but she'll be someone at tonight's ball."

A flicker of apprehension came over Toby. That soon? With a bravado he didn't feel, he laughed. "Tonight? Why the rush?"

"To make sure you don't have time to warn her."

Unfortunately, his answer made too much sense to argue, and he'd come too far into this to back out now. "Fine. Tonight. I'll pick the lady and the wager will be set."

Pennella offered a curt nod. "Very well. And if you fail to show up, you forfeit and your estate will be mine."

"I'll be there."

Toby wasn't able to relax until Pennella left White's. As he settled back into his seat, the gentlemen in the room turned their attention back to what they'd been doing before Pennella disrupted everything.

Orlando tapped the cards in his hands and gave him a look that indicated he wanted to say something but wasn't sure if he should.

Toby reluctantly picked up his cards and answered, "You don't have to say it. I should have kept my mouth shut instead of goading Pennella along."

"He was determined to make a wager with someone in the room."

"Yes, I gathered that much, but I didn't have to take the bait."

"He didn't give you a choice. Anyone listening could see what was going on."

Running his fingers along the edges of the cards, Toby thought over how he could have done things differently. "Well, I'm stuck now. The best I can do is minimize the damage from here."

"Do you have a lady in mind for the wager?"

"No. I'm just going to pick someone who isn't likely to choose Pennella."

"That's not going to be easy. He can be charming when he wants to be."

"So I hear." Though he heard the gentleman couldn't keep a mistress for longer than a few months, so he couldn't be that charming. He placed his cards on the table. "I don't feel like playing."

"I don't blame you. I wouldn't either if I were in your shoes. Do you want to get out of here?"

Toby nodded, and they put everything away before heading out. He ignored the way the other gentlemen watched him, no doubt wondering what he'd do now that he'd made such an outrageous wager with Pennella. They probably thought he was going to lose. No one wagered anything with Pennella and won. And except for Edon who never lost a single game, they would be right.

Once they were a block away from White's, Toby released his breath. "I need your help finding a lady tonight."

His friend shook his head. "I don't know what good I can do."

"I don't have to pick a lady as soon as I enter the ballroom. I'll have some time to dance with a few of them. Then I'll find out if there's one who doesn't seem easy to impress."

"Don't you want someone who is easy to impress?"

"Not to the point where she'll fall at Pennella's feet."

"Ah, then you want a lady who's intelligent."

Toby's lips curled up at his friend's joke. If nothing else could be said for Orlando, he could make him laugh no matter how dire the situation. "Yes, a lady who is smart enough to see through Pennella's flattery. If we both dance with the ladies in their first Season, we should be able to find one who has a good chance of not picking him."

"If that's the case, then you should select one you'd like to marry."

"No, that's of no consequence. After I win the bet, I won't hold her to the proposal."

"Aren't you interested in Pennella's estate?"

"The only thing I want is for Pennella to leave me alone."

"Even though you could use the money?" When Toby shook his head, he added, "What if we pick a lady who's wealthy? You could marry her and get the money you need."

"It wouldn't feel right."

"Why? Gentlemen marry for money all the time. Also, you have a title, something ladies seek. This could be something both of you could win if you tell her upfront what's going on. Tell her as a secret, of course. That way no one is the wiser."

"You know I can't tell her about the wager. Pennella's not allowed to reveal the truth to her anymore than I can."

"I suppose, though it's a shame you can't work out some kind of bargain."

Yes, it was a shame. But there was still a chance that things could work out, and he would do his part to tip the scale in his favor. "So, will you help me find an intelligent lady?"

"Yes, I'll do what I can."

"Thank you."

With Orlando's help, he had a good chance of finding the perfect lady.

Chapter Two

Miss Regina Giles turned away from her mother. If she wasn't careful, she'd end up with a headache. Her mother meant well. She knew she did, but all the fuss was getting to be too much.

"Would you like more tea, my dear?" her mother called out from where she and her two friends sat in the drawing room.

Regina continued to stare out the window. "No thanks, Mother. I've had enough."

"It's probably nerves," one of her mother's friends said. "This being her first Season and all, there's a lot of pressure for her to find a respectable husband."

"Oh, she won't just find a respectable husband," her mother began in a tone that left no room for argument. "She's going to marry a titled gentleman."

"A titled one?" another lady asked, sounding as impressed as Regina knew her mother hoped she'd be.

"Most assuredly. Her father and I will have nothing but the best for her. Her son will one day have a title."

With a heavy sigh, Regina tuned them out as they continued to talk about her future as if she had nothing to do with it. Her mother was ambitious, had always been that way. It was why her mother married her father when she realized he had the potential to make a significant amount of money. Whether or not her mother and father loved each other, she didn't know. They were amiable enough, but they spent most of their time apart. Her father went out to make more money, and her mother was more than happy to spend it then turn around and show off her new things to her socially influential friends.

Pressing her forehead against the window, Regina closed her eyes. She inhaled, held her breath, and slowly exhaled. The exercise often calmed her nerves. It was already June, and she was no closer to securing a husband than when her Season had started. This didn't bode well. She needed a husband—one with a title—before the Season ended. If she didn't... She didn't want to think about it.

"Regina?" her mother called out.

Opening her eyes, she turned around. "Yes?"

"We need to get ready to leave, my dear. I want to stop by a dress shop before we have someone decorate your hair for tonight's ball." She rose to her feet and smiled at her friends. "She's beautiful already, of course, but sometimes gentlemen require a little extra to catch their attention."

"Oh, that's for sure," one of her friends agreed. "Their minds are often on what they can see." She gave them a wink and giggled.

Regina didn't understand the joke but then decided she didn't care. The ladies lauded appearances above all else, and apparently, gentlemen thought the same way.

Her mother came over to her and touched her wavy blonde hair. "I wonder how you'd look with pearls in your hair? Pearls are lovely." She patted her shoulder and grinned. "Only the best for you. Mark my word, you'll be the most beautiful lady at the ball."

Regina swallowed the lump in her throat and nodded. In one way, she wanted to finally attract a titled gentleman to satisfy her mother, but she also feared what it meant. Though most married ladies never showed any signs of discontent, she wondered if being under a husband's thumb would be all that different from living under her mother's.

Her mother turned back to her friends. "Thank you for the tea and scones."

Regina repeated the sentiment and followed her mother out of the room, hoping tonight would go as well as her mother planned.

"THEN THERE'S THE MUSEUM, of course, but who wants to spend their time doing something so boring?" the pretty brunette rambled as she danced with Toby that evening at the ball. "There are other things we could be doing with our time, and I intend to go out and do it."

Toby offered a polite smile. He doubted he'd win the wager if he picked her. She'd probably fall in love with Pennella as soon as she met him. Pennella loved to travel. A couple months ago, he'd come to White's and bragged about going to a bullfight in Spain. He even got to meet the matador who fought the bull. Even now, Toby resisted the urge to roll his eyes. All Pennella ever did was brag about places he'd visited, money he spent, and people he met.

This lady, no doubt, would just love all his stories. And that made her unsuitable for the bet. Not to mention the fact that Toby had no desire to engage in any of the things she enjoyed. He much preferred the safety of his chair to the idea of going to Africa to see lions in person. No. She wouldn't be happy with him, and she'd sense that right away and pick Pennella before the wager officially started.

The dance came to an end, allowing Toby a much needed reprieve. He bowed to her, thanked her for a lovely dance, and headed for the punch table where Orlando stood.

"Any luck?" Orlando asked.

"No. How about you?"

"No. Unless you fancy a lady who mumbles all the time."

He winced and shook his head.

Orlando grinned. "Don't despair. The evening is still young, and we just got started."

"I envy your ability to look at the best in every situation."

They watched the couples on the dance floor, and Orlando pointed to a dashing brunette who laughed at something her dance partner said. "What do you think of her?"

Toby considered her and saw her give another gentleman a wink. "I don't think so."

"Why not? She's one of the prettier ladies at this ball."

"While that's true, I don't think she's the best choice." Maybe it didn't matter who the lady he selected was, but he preferred one who wasn't extending a welcome to every gentleman in the room. He scanned the room and saw a raven-haired beauty. "What about her?"

"She might do. Want to dance with her?"

Toby nodded but then caught sight of a pretty blonde who looked bored. "Wait. I think I'll dance with her."

"Why? She's not as beautiful as the brunette."

"I disagree. She's more attractive, but that's not why I want to dance with her. There's something about her that seems," for lack of a better word, he shrugged, "different."

Orlando laughed. "Different?"

"I can't explain it."

"All right. I'll dance with the better looking of the two."

Amused at his friend's teasing tone, Toby waited for the music to end before making his way through the crowded room. He had to call out to her so she wouldn't leave the dance floor. She turned in his direction, and he was struck by the way her eyes flashed the most brilliant shade of green.

He cleared his throat and offered a bow. "May I have the pleasure of the next dance?"

She hesitated for a moment then curtsied. "Yes, you may."

"I hope you don't mind dancing with me."

"Pardon?"

"I notice you only agreed to dance with me to be polite."

The music began and both fell into step.

She shrugged. "It doesn't seem that anyone here cares much about anything, except to make an impression."

"Most people come here for that," he admitted, "though some are sincere about finding a husband or wife."

"Is that why you're here?"

"I wouldn't mind finding a nice lady to marry." And that was the truth, even if it wasn't something he was doing at the moment. "Are you here to find a husband?"

"I have to find a husband."

"Have to?"

"My mother is insistent on it. It's her grand dream, and if I fail to snare one this Season, it might be the death of her."

Noting her humor, he laughed. "What children go through to appease their mothers."

"Well, we owe it to them, or at least I owe it to mine. If it wasn't for her, I would never have been born."

"You possess marvelous wit, Miss...?"

"Giles. And you are?"

"Lord Davenport." He hesitated to ask her more questions, but of all the ladies he'd met tonight, she seemed like the most promising one. "Tell me, Miss Giles, what is it you're looking for in a husband?"

"My mother's demands are that he have a title, is well-educated, and has a good reputation with the Ton."

"I didn't ask what your mother wanted. I asked what you wanted," he pointed out with a smile.

"My opinion makes no difference."

"It should make all the difference in the world. You're the one who is getting married."

Chuckling, she said, "Come now, my lord. You know how things are. Ladies are to marry a titled gentleman, and the titled gentleman is to marry the lady who has the most money."

"Well, a lady with money is a huge benefit, especially if the titled gentleman came upon hard times."

"Then we are in agreement. Money and a title are the reasons any of us parade ourselves through these balls."

He forced himself to laugh instead of wince. She was brutally honest. It wouldn't be very noble of him to pick her. If he was a decent gentleman, he'd pick someone else. But he doubted she'd ever pick Pennella, and for what he needed, she was perfect.

The dance came to an end, so he bowed to her. "It's been a pleasure, Miss Giles. I hope our paths will cross again."

She curtsied. "Lord Davenport."

He sensed she had enjoyed their dance. Maybe not as much as he did but maybe enough to agree to go to Hyde Park with him. That would be the first place he'd take her if she agreed. But first, he had to find Pennella and tell him he selected her for the wager.

He found Orlando talking to the brunette he had chosen to dance with. "You're wrong, Miss Boyle," Orlando said. "Your hair is lovely. Far more so than any of the other brunettes in this room."

Surprised, Toby's eyebrows raised in interest. Since when did Orlando take note of a lady's hair color?

"You flatter me, my lord."

"Only because you deserve to be flattered."

Toby wasn't opposed to romance, but the way the two gushed over each other was enough to make him nauseous. Thankfully, another gentleman came over to ask her to dance, so Orlando had to leave her side. Toby doubted he would have left otherwise.

"So, how did it go?" Orlando asked him.

"I could ask you the same thing, but I already know the answer to that." Glancing at Miss Boyle who curtsied and shot the new gentleman a coy smile, he shook his head. "She flatters everyone she dances with, not just you."

"That doesn't mean I couldn't enjoy talking to her. This is her first Season, and she's looking for a husband."

"Oh, well in that case, it's only natural she goes around and charms every gentleman she gets her hands on."

Shooting him an amused smile, Orlando said, "She's trying hard to secure a husband. I suspect she needs money."

"Oh, so anyone with a good amount of money will do. How nice it is to know she'll choose you if you come with a large enough estate."

"I fail to see what is wrong with her motivation when you and Pennella have that wager going. At least she will give her husband an heir. If Pennella wins the wager, he'll give the lady in question a life of misery. If you win, you'll give her an estate your father left in ruins. That is, of course, if you don't end the engagement. It seems to me, that Miss Boyle is being far too kind."

"I hate the fact that you can argue anything to your advantage," he grumbled.

Orlando chuckled. "Now, how did your dance go?"

"Better than I expected."

"Does that mean you've selected your lady?"

"I have. Her name is Miss Giles. She's a bit of a cynic, but she has a good point. Gentlemen are looking for money, and ladies want a gentleman with a title."

"Are you sure Miss Giles is the one?"

"Yes, I am."

"Good. Then let's find Pennella, Edon and Ashbourne to make it official."

Chapter Three

"I found her," Toby told Pennella.

Behind Toby were Lord Edon and Mr. Robinson. When Pennella turned to face him, Toby motioned to Miss Giles who was dancing.

"That's the lady you want?" Pennella asked, scanning her with a critical eye.

"Yes," Toby said. He turned to Edon and Mr. Robinson. "As agreed, I'm allowed to choose the lady, and she's the one I pick."

"She's not as pretty as what I'm used to," Pennella began, "but I suppose she'll do."

Toby bit back the urge to say that she was a beautiful lady. Maybe if Pennella didn't fancy her, he wouldn't strive so hard to win her hand. Noting the expectation in Pennella's eyes, Toby realized it didn't matter whether he fancied her or not. He'd do everything he could to get her to choose him. He could only hope he understood her, that she wasn't easily given to flattery.

"Then it's agreed," Pennella told Edon and Mr. Robinson. "Whoever Miss Giles chooses wins the wager. We'll sign the agreement before we leave the ball tonight."

The two gentlemen indicated their agreement before they returned to their dance partners.

Pennella looked at Toby with raised eyebrows. "You won't mind if I dance with her since you already had your turn?"

Toby wondered if Pennella had been watching him, and sure enough, he had. "Of course not," he forced out, offering a polite smile.

With a nod, Pennella waited until the music ended then made his way over to her. Already, Toby's gut tensed. This was a bad idea. There was no way this wager was going to end well. If only he hadn't stepped into Pennella's trap.

Unable to stop him, Toby watched as he bowed to her, using that confident smile that bothered him to no end. She curtsied and accepted his hand. The two began to dance and the knot in his gut tightened. He couldn't step in and stop it. He had to stand along the edge of the dance floor and watch as Pennella talked to her.

His eyebrows furrowed. Did she enjoy listening to him? From his vantage point, it was hard to tell if she was smiling at Pennella the same way she'd smiled at him. As Orlando approached, he gestured toward her. "Does she look happy?"

Orlando shrugged. "It's hard to say. That's the same smile she gave you."

Hiding his scowl, he returned his gaze to her. That was horrible. If she was giving his nemesis the same smile she gave him, then he had no advantage. At least not yet. He had to remind himself that this was only the first meeting. He'd see her again. All he had to do was secure a time and place to meet with her. And he'd do that before the night was over.

"I DON'T MEAN TO BE forward, but you are one of the most beautiful ladies at this ball," Lord Pennella said.

Regina twirled in time to the music and rolled her eyes. A glance at her mother warned her that she better be nice. When she faced him again, she forced herself to smile.

"What is it you want?" she asked. Her mother would never approve of the question, but she was tired after spending all evening going from one gentleman to another. All she wanted to do was go home and rest in bed.

"I wanted to dance with the best looking lady in the room," he replied, flashing her a smile she suspected was supposed to be charming. "Now that I'm dancing with you, my evening is complete."

"Thank you." She only said it because she was expected to. Soon the dance would be over. With any luck, he wouldn't ask for another one. She had so little patience with deceit.

"Do you ever visit the museum?"

This wasn't something she wanted to answer because she was afraid of where it was leading. Her mother would be delighted to no end, especially since he had a title. As it was, she had yet to secure the interest of any titled gentleman in the room, and she could tell by the way her mother anxiously fanned herself that she was getting impatient. Taking a deep breath, she forced out, "Yes, I have on occasion."

"Do you enjoy going there?"

"Sometimes."

"I'd love to go with you in three days. I hear a new portrait is arriving then."

She released her breath and glanced at her mother. "I'd be honored, my lord."

The music came to an end, and he bowed, his smile wide. "I look forward to seeing you again, Miss Giles."

With a forced smile, she returned the sentiment then hurried over to her mother. She was exhausted. Her feet hurt, and she was unbearably hot. All she wanted to do was curl up in bed and go to sleep.

"How did that last dance go?" her mother asked.

"He wishes to see me again."

"Is he a titled gentleman?"

"Yes, he's Lord Pennella."

"Splendid!"

"In three days we will go to the museum."

Letting out a delightful laugh, she finally stopped waving her fan. "This is so exciting! We must think of what you can talk to him about so you don't lose his interest."

"I don't think that will be hard to do. He seemed rather intent on speaking about himself. As long as you ask him questions, he should be more than happy to talk."

"That can be said about any gentleman, Regina." She gasped and leaned toward her. "Another gentleman is coming over here. You danced with him earlier."

Curious, she turned around, surprised when she saw Lord Davenport. She offered a hesitant smile. "Lord Davenport, this is my mother."

"It's a pleasure to meet you, my lord," her mother said with a curtsy.

He bowed and glanced at Regina. "May I share another dance with you?"

She looked at her mother who gave her an encouraging nod. With a smile, she extended her hand. "It'd be my pleasure."

And surprisingly, she thought this dance wouldn't be as burdensome as the others, probably because he was the one gentleman she'd been able to speak freely to. Perhaps he might be one of the few people who could accept her brazen honesty.

The orchestra began to play, and she moved in time with him to the music.

"How has your evening been since we last talked?" he asked.

"Well, I managed to stay awake," she joked.

He smiled. "That's always good. It wouldn't be good if you fell asleep while dancing."

"I'd say not. Mother would never forgive me for ruining this dress by falling onto the floor."

Chuckling, he said, "If you happen to fall asleep while we're dancing, I'll catch you so your dress will be safe."

She laughed, impressed by his wit. "Then I'm in good hands."

"Always and forever."

Amused, she asked, "Always and forever? That's a long time."

"Then it's a good thing I'm a patient gentleman."

"If I said you have a refreshing sense of humor, would you think more highly of yourself than you ought?"

"No, but I might take it as an indication that you'd go for a walk with me at Hyde Park."

Her skin flushed with pleasure. Up to now, she hadn't wanted to see any of the gentlemen she'd met again, but she did want to see him. "My mother would chaperone," she replied, choosing her words carefully, "and she's likely to be a little...enthusiastic about it."

"When you say 'enthusiastic', do you mean obnoxious?"

"Maybe I'm the only one who sees her that way, but yes, that is what I mean. She's likely to hint insistently about marriage. You have no need to fear that's my aim. It's hers."

"You already told me that's her goal for you. I'm sure I can handle her."

"Well, if you feel brave enough to risk it, then I'll be happy to take a walk with you."

She couldn't be sure, but she thought he seemed relieved. What a curious gentleman he was. He hadn't been deterred by her honesty, and even better, the threat of her mother hadn't scared him away. Of all the gentlemen she'd met this Season, he was, by far, the most intriguing one.

The music stopped all too soon, and as sorry as she was to see the dance come to an end, she couldn't deny the flicker of excitement that came over her as he suggested walking in two days' time.

"I'm looking forward to walking with you, Miss Giles," he said with a bow.

"We'll see if you can say that after spending the afternoon with my mother," she joked as she curtsied, pleased when he chuckled.

She turned and went to her mother whose eyebrows were raised in undeniable interest. "That seemed to go well," her mother said, her gaze still on him as he went to talk to another gentleman.

"Mother, please don't stare."

"You mustn't be embarrassed. I didn't get a good enough look at him while you were dancing."

"I think you got a good look. You're just being a busybody again."

Offering a slight shrug, she opened her fan and waved it. "And what if I am? You're my only child. Of course, I'm interested in what happens to you." She bit her lower lip then asked, "Was he a titled gentleman?"

"Yes."

"And he came over to you to dance with you twice?"

Noting the gleam in her eye, Regina sighed. "In two days, he wishes to take me for a walk in Hyde Park."

As she expected, her mother let out a squeal of delight. "Marvelous! Two gentlemen vying for your hand!"

"Don't get excited. Lord Pennella and Lord Davenport are only taking me to the museum and to Hyde Park. Nothing more may come of it."

"It will if you're careful. I'm going to have Lady Seyton come by."

She gagged. "Not her again."

"She got you this far, and her reputation is excellent. Everyone Lady Seyton has taught secured a husband in one Season. You can't go wrong with her." Regina sighed, and her mother took her by the arm and led her out of the ballroom. "We have a long day ahead of us tomorrow. You must get a good night's sleep."

There was no point in arguing with her, and besides, she was exhausted and wanted nothing more than to go to bed.

Chapter Four

"Get ready to hand over your estate, Davenport," a familiarly irritating voice called out at White's the next day.

It wasn't a question of if Toby had to look. The question was how could he appear appropriately bored. With a long sigh, he lowered his cards and glanced over his shoulder, making a big show of trying not to yawn.

Not to be discouraged, Pennella strutted up to him like a proud peacock. Then he sat next to Toby. "It's a shame you didn't pick a lady who would be more challenging. In only one dance, I secured an afternoon with her at the museum. We'll go there in two days."

"That long?" Toby glanced at Orlando who hid his grin behind his cards.

Pennella's eyebrows furrowed. "What do you mean 'that long'? Considering I only met her last evening, I wouldn't say that's a long time."

"I meant I'm surprised it took you that long to get her to see you again. She agreed to go to Hyde Park with me tomorrow."

His boast was rewarded with a round of laughter from the other gentlemen in the room. He would have taken delight in it had it not been for the scowl on Pennella's face. It was a bold move to challenge him, especially in front of gentlemen. But he didn't dare show any signs of weakness.

"Things just got a lot more interesting," Lord Toplyn said, walking over to them. "The lady in question has agreed to let both of you call on her. I don't know about anyone else," he glanced at the others, "but I'd like to make a little wager on the wager. A hundred pounds says Davenport wins."

"A foolish bet," Lord Haynes snorted. "Pennella has more ladies vying for his affections than anyone in this room except for Edon."

"I've changed my life since I got married," Edon called out from where he sat with Mr. Robinson.

"Thereby allowing Pennella to replace you as London's most notorious rake," Toplyn countered, earning another round of chuckles.

"If you think a lady's easily impressed by a rake," Edon began, "you have another thing coming."

"Your wife regrets marrying you?" Toplyn asked.

"She was crying on their wedding day," Mr. Robinson spoke up.

"Oh, go on and bet," Orlando called out to them.

While the gentlemen gathered around them to make their bets, Pennella leaned toward him. "I wouldn't get my hopes up. I'm the one who suggested we meet in two days."

Ignoring the gentlemen who gathered around a ledger to make their bets, Toby put his cards down and shot his friend a pointed gaze. "Just what was all that about?"

"What was 'what' about?" Orlando asked.

"You know very well what I'm talking about. Why did you encourage them," he motioned to the gentlemen, "to make a bet?"

"They were going to do it anyway. Besides," he shrugged, "it got their attention off of you and Pennella. That is what you wanted, wasn't it?"

"Well, yes..."

"So I did you a favor. There's no need to thank me." He glanced at his pocket watch and stood up. "I should go. Remember that attractive brunette I danced with when you danced with Miss Giles?"

"The one who was flirting with every gentleman who came near her?"

"Yes, that's the one. I'm going to make it a point to see her again. She told me she's going to be taking a nice stroll in the market today."

"And she specified a time?"

"She might have mentioned being there around two."

"I don't understand why you're so fascinated with her. She'd probably do that with any gentleman who shows her any interest."

"Yes, and I'm dying to find out why."

Toby watched as Orlando left the room. He debated whether or not he should stay there but then decided he'd rather not witness the group of gentlemen who were writing down their bids into the book. Whether most were choosing him or Pennella, he didn't care. The only thing he cared about was making sure Miss Giles didn't choose Pennella because if she did, Pennella would toss her aside like he discarded mistresses. Sure, he'd give her his name and ensure an heir with her, but he would never treat her as a lady. Toby already made the mistake of getting involved in this stupid wager. Whatever he had to do, he would make sure Miss Giles chose him instead of Pennella. Then he'd release her from any obligation to marry him. Only then would his conscience be clear.

"YOU'LL NEED TO SMILE at anything he says, no matter how boring it may be," Lady Seyton instructed as she paced back and forth in her drawing room.

"I understand," Regina replied. That wasn't shocking. Who'd want to keep talking to someone who yawned at whatever they said?

"Indeed," her mother chimed in with an overenthusiastic nod. "The goal is to get him to marry you. Once you succeed in that, you can fall asleep while he talks."

"Or you can leave the room," Lady Seyton offered a wicked smile. "Even while he's still talking."

Her mother laughed. "Oh, you are a sly one, my lady."

"Once you're married, you no longer have to concern yourself with making him feel as if he's important," she added. "Give him an heir and the rest is done. Then you are free to spend his money on beautiful gowns and jewels while you go to the ball or to the theatre or wherever else. Gentlemen do have their uses if they come with the right amount of money."

"Agreed," her mother said. "There's no point in marrying if you can't live a life of comfort."

"And it's even better if you rarely see him."

Regina gave a hesitant smile while the two ladies laughed. What was the point in getting married if the goal was to spend as much time apart from her husband as possible? It seemed like a lonely way to live. With a sigh, she picked up her cup of tea and drank it for no other reason than to have something to do besides feign merriment over this conversation.

"Securing a titled gentleman isn't really that hard," Lady Seyton continued. "All gentlemen want to be important. It's in their blood. Even if he's not a king of a country, he wants to be the king of his home. Make him think that you adore him, and when you snap your fingers, he'll come running to do your bidding. A simple compliment here and there can do wonders."

"What if there's nothing to compliment?" her mother asked.

"Oh, there's always something."

"What if he laughs like a hyena?"

"Tell him he has a marvelous sense of humor to find things he can laugh about. 'It's a gift, my lord, to find pleasure in the things around you.'"

This earned another round of giggles.

Regina forced a light chuckle. Her father wasn't a titled gentleman, but he had accumulated significant wealth. No doubt it was his wealth that made her mother happy.

Though it was a shame, it wasn't uncommon. Most gentlemen sought some gain from a marriage, as did most ladies. She couldn't fault them for it. And being the only child, Regina would give her future husband a sizable inheritance. It put her in an ideal position, really. She had her pick of titled gentlemen. Already two were showing an interest in her. She should be enjoying the whole process of picking the gentleman she fancied. But wasn't it peculiar that in one evening two expressed an interest in her? She hadn't gathered any real interest up to now.

Well, there was Lord Nestleton who asked to see her three times, but during that third visit, it became apparent he preferred her mother. She had to hand it to her mother. She put a stop to the nonsense at once. At least, her mother was a faithful wife.

"You can do better than him," her mother said after she told Lord Nestleton to leave. "Titled gentlemen are everywhere. You miss one, another will come by."

And now it seemed as if her mother's foresight had paid off.

"Regina," her mother said, breaking her from her thoughts.

She looked at her mother.

"Lady Seyton asked you to stand up," her mother continued.

Regina rose to her feet and faced the lady.

"Walk from that side of the room to the other," Lady Seyton instructed, pointing from the closed door to the window.

Her eyebrows furrowed. What did walking have to do with getting a gentleman to propose? She thought to ask this, but the expectant look on her mother's face stopped her. With a nod, she went to the door and traveled across the room. When she reached the window, she turned toward Lady Seyton who slightly frowned.

"Your walk isn't bad," she began as she tapped her finger on her lips. "But there's room for improvement."

"Which is true with anything," her mother added. "No matter how much we polish our skills, we can always polish them up a little more."

"Yes, that's true." She strode over to Regina and studied her. "You have wonderful posture. I can tell you're trying hard to please your mother."

At that, her mother's face lit up in pleasure. The silent action startled Regina. She had no idea her mother cared if she tried to please her or not.

"Let's try tilting your chin a little higher," Lady Seyton said. "Not too high, you understand. You don't want people to think you're arrogant. Here." She placed her finger under Regina's chin and lifted it so slightly that Regina had trouble telling the difference. "Then let's put your shoulders back like this." She adjusted her shoulders. "And then straighten your back a tad." She pressed into the small of her back. "There. It doesn't hurt to show off your best assets." She winked.

It took Regina a moment to realize the lady was referring to her breasts which stood out more than before. Her face grew warm. Gentlemen didn't really spend their time looking at a lady's breasts, did they?

"Good." Lady Seyton spun around so that her back was to her. "When you walk, give a slight swing to your hips. You don't want to be obvious, of course. You want to give a hint. Make him think of more intimate matters." She proceeded to stroll to the door, demonstrating the technique which Regina had to admit had a certain amount of grace to it. "Even if you don't love him and he doesn't love you, he'll want to visit you in bed from time to time. If you can turn his mind in that direction, you'll have an easier time securing the proposal." She clapped her hands and gestured to her. "Now, you try it. Walk."

Despite the butterflies fluttering in her stomach, she obeyed. The last thing she wanted either Lord Pennella or Lord Davenport thinking about when she saw them was having her in their bed. She glanced at her mother to see if she approved of this, but her mother seemed content as she sipped her tea.

"Much better," Lady Seyton said when Regina reached her at the door. In a whisper, she added, "You have a good bosom. The gentlemen vying for your hand will like what they see."

Her jaw dropped as Lady Seyton turned her attention to her mother. "Your daughter has an excellent chance of securing a proposal within a month. She's graceful, polite, quiet, and beautiful. I don't think there's anything else I can teach her."

"Splendid." Her mother put her cup down and stood from the settee. "What do I owe you?"

"Twenty pounds will suffice."

As her mother took the money out of her reticule, Regina breathed a sigh of relief. Maybe now her mother would stop the lessons.

After her mother thanked Lady Seyton, she led Regina out of the house. "You've done very well, my dear," her mother said, her smile wide. "I don't believe in bragging, but I have one of the finest ladies in London for a daughter."

"Really?" Regina's steps slowed as she studied her mother, hardly believing her ears.

"Don't look at me like that. While I don't often say it, I've always been proud of you. From the moment you were born, I knew you were special."

"I'm sure all mothers think that of their daughters."

"They may think it, but I know it."

Pleased, she smiled. "Thank you, Mother."

"Don't thank me until you're married and living in a grand estate surrounded by exquisite gowns, jewelry, and servants."

"There's more to life than money."

"But money certainly helps. Take it from someone who knows."

Well, it didn't matter if her mother couldn't believe someone could be happy without a lot of money. The point was, she chose to give her several compliments that day. And that was something Regina never thought she'd do.

Chapter Five

Toby stepped out of his carriage and took a good look at Miss Giles' townhouse. He didn't know why the thought of seeing her should make his heart leap in anticipation. Yes, she'd been utterly charming at the ball, but he wasn't here to secure a marriage. Quite the opposite, he was going to prevent her from spending the rest of her life with an unsuitable gentleman.

And that included him. He was no better than the gentlemen she'd mentioned who wanted to marry for money. But he wouldn't marry her. He would set her free to marry someone who deserved her. Enjoying his time with her was merely his reward for doing the right thing.

He made his way up the steps to the front door and knocked on it. Glancing at the sky, he thought it'd be a good day for a walk. While there were a few clouds, there was no indication that it would rain. Even better, a cool breeze was perfect for the summer day.

The footman opened the door.

Toby smiled. "Good afternoon. I'm here to see Miss Giles."

"She's expecting you. Come this way."

As he stepped into the entryway, he took note of the immaculate condition of the townhouse. Undoubtedly, her family had enough servants to meet their every need. He didn't fare nearly as well. If she knew he could only afford a butler, she'd be appalled.

When the footman brought him to the drawing room, he had to stop himself from staring at the fine furnishings. All brand new. All the current style. Even the drapes and rugs didn't have years of wear and tear on them.

The butler brought in a tray full of tea and scones. The tray didn't have a single scratch on it. Was it possible that everything in this place was brand new, or did this family take great care with their possessions?

"It's a pleasure to see you again, my lord."

Forcing his attention off the solid oak table the butler set the tray on, he saw Miss Giles curtsy. She was absolutely breathtaking. Despite what Orlando thought, there was nothing common about her. She had a captivating look, one that was the perfect blend of sweetness and seduction. He bet she had a passionate spark simmering beneath her polite exterior.

Shifting his thoughts back to appropriate matters, he bowed. "The pleasure is mine, I assure you."

She gestured to the chair. "Please have a seat. My mother will be here shortly. Then we can go for a walk."

"You have a lovely place," he said as he obeyed and sat in a plush chair that hadn't seen years of use. "I'm glad you agreed to walk with me."

"Well, you were one of the few people I've ever met who didn't take off running when I showed my cynical side."

He chuckled at her joke. "It takes more than someone pointing out the truth to scare me away."

"Don't tell me you've come across other ladies who are as cynical as I am."

Catching the teasing tone in her voice, he chuckled. "No, I won't tell you that. But it is refreshing to find a lady who isn't obsessed with finding a titled gentleman."

"I think parents are more obsessed with it than most ladies are."

"You're telling me ladies don't dream of being a countess or a duchess?"

"Sure. But not every single lady out there wants to be one. It's a lot of responsibility. And who knows if she can guarantee her husband an heir?"

"Does that worry you?"

With a shrug, she adjusted her gloves. "If the gentleman has a daughter, no one blames him for it. They blame his wife for failing to give him an heir. If he gets a son, they congratulate him."

"So your hesitation about marrying a titled gentleman has to do with the fear you might not have a son?"

"Wouldn't that upset the gentleman I marry?"

"That depends on the gentleman. As you said, not every single lady desires a titled gentleman. Likewise, not all gentlemen require their wives to give them a son."

"And what of you, Lord Davenport? Do you require a son?"

"No," he softly said, "I don't."

She studied him for a moment then poured him a cup of tea and handed it to him. "I'll take it for granted you're telling me the truth. You seem to be the honest sort."

He managed not to wince at her compliment. What would she think of him if she knew about the wager? Nothing positive, he was sure. Clearing his throat, he thanked her for the tea and sipped it as she added a spoonful of sugar to hers, leaning forward as she did so. It was highly improper, but his gaze lingered on the hint of cleavage her position allowed. When she straightened back up, he shifted in the chair to hide the evidence of his attraction to her. If he wasn't careful, she'd know exactly what he'd been thinking. And he didn't want that.

"Well," she began before she sipped her tea, "since you're brave enough to take a walk with me and my mother, it's only fair I warn you that she's likely to ask you all kinds of questions about who you know. She also follows the latest gossip and might try to wiggle some juicy tidbit from you. My suggestion is to claim ignorance to everything."

"I take it you don't delight in gossip?"

"I don't. I find it a horrible pastime. Why people can't stick with matters that only concern them, I'll never understand."

If only she knew she had become the unwilling victim in a wager at White's! Forcing aside the stab of guilt that pricked him, he drank more tea. "It's certainly a pleasant day."

"Yes, the air coming in through the window is refreshing. Sometimes I feel restless when I'm indoors."

"Do you?"

"It's not just because of my mother," she said with a grin. "I like being outside and enjoying life."

"Do you enjoy the theatre and circus?"

"No. When I said I like being outside, I meant outside of any building. My mother prefers to take a stroll through the market, but I actually prefer Hyde Park or out in the country. There's nothing more peaceful."

As he drank his tea, he came to the shocking conclusion that he liked her. Liked her immensely, in fact. She was like a breath of fresh air. Not shy in the least when it came to stating her mind, something much needed in a society that prided itself on sticking with a formal politeness that came with constant backstabbing.

And though she didn't let anyone close to her right away, he suspected that once she did, a gentleman would have a faithful companion for the rest of his life. He could trust that what she told him to his face was what she'd say about him behind his back. There was no deception with her. He finished the tea and tried not to wince. If she knew about him, she'd throw him right out of her townhouse...and her life.

"Lord Davenport, I presume?" came a lady's melodic voice.

Setting the tea down, he rose to his feet in time for Miss Giles to say, "My lord, you remember my mother, Mrs. Giles."

He bowed. "It's a pleasure."

She curtsied and smiled. "Likewise, my lord. It's my understanding that we are going to take a lovely stroll through the park."

"Yes," he replied, glancing at Miss Giles who placed her cup on the tray and stood up. "Your daughter mentioned it."

"If you wish, we could do something more to your liking," Mrs. Giles offered.

"No. A stroll suits me just fine. The day is a beautiful one." Almost as lovely as Miss Giles, but not quite. It was hard to match her particular beauty and grace.

Her mother's smile widened. "Excellent."

Taking that as his cue, he said, "My carriage is outside."

He followed the ladies outside, and while they walked down the steps, he couldn't help but appreciate the nice curves Miss Giles possessed. She wasn't a stick of a lady. No. She had a full bosom and hips. Charming wit and a wonderful figure. A gentleman couldn't do better than this.

In that instant, he made his decision. He would go through with the wager and marry her, if she chose him over Pennella.

As they rode to the park, he was grateful that of all the things he owned, he made sure to splurge for a good carriage. He hated to think of Miss Giles' reaction when she realized his estate was in trouble. But hopefully—God willing—she wouldn't mind it so much since he loved her. Maybe love could cover up a multitude of flaws.

After they arrived at the park, he was surprised when her mother started pointing out all the people they passed, providing surprising details about them. It seemed the lady knew almost everything there was to know about anyone. She knew who had a title, how long their family had it, what their interests were, and a few stories she'd heard about them.

At one point, he wondered just how much she knew about him, and his gut tightened in apprehension. But then Miss Giles caught his attention and rolled her eyes, a silent "see what I mean about my mother gossiping?" message. If her mother knew about him, it seemed that it didn't bother either Miss Giles or her mother one bit. He relaxed

"Of course, I don't know if it's true that the Duke of Rumsey threatened Lord Edon with a sword," Mrs. Giles continued rambling after they passed Lord and Lady Edon. "But I will say that Lord Edon cleaned up his act. He doesn't engage in scandalous behaviors anymore. At least, I haven't heard of any. Have you, Lord Davenport?"

Not expecting her to stop, Toby had to think over what she'd been talking about so he could properly answer her question. "No, I haven't heard of Lord Edon engaging in scandalous activities ever since he got married."

"I didn't think so. His Grace must have put the fear of the devil into him," she replied, her expression thoughtful. "Tell me, my lord," she continued, "what is Lord Edon really like?"

"Mother," Miss Giles spoke up, "I don't see what good it does to speculate about Lord Edon. Let him be at peace."

"Oh, you're so serious about everything," her mother said with a sigh. "All winter long I'm cooped up in the country with nothing to entertain me. I come to London to enjoy myself, and part of that is engaging with others."

"Engaging with others is fine," her daughter replied. "Being your own version of the *Tittletattle* is something else."

Toby's lips curled up as Miss Giles compared her mother to the scandal sheets.

"I have to make it a point to know who these people are," Mrs. Giles insisted, giving her daughter a pointed gaze. "You should only marry an appropriate gentleman."

At that, Miss Giles' face turned pink. "Then why not discuss only single gentlemen? Why talk about Lord Edon who is already taken?"

"You're right, dear," her mother consented. But before Miss Giles had a chance to relax, her mother asked, "Who would you like to discuss?"

Toby noted the exasperation on Miss Giles' face and almost laughed. But he managed to cover it up with a cough. Then, in hopes of making things easier for her, he said, "I hear Mr. Hastings is a fine opera singer. Word is he's worth listening to at least once while in London. Have you had the pleasure of going to see him yet?"

"As a matter of fact, I have," Mrs. Giles said, her face lighting up. "My daughter and I make it a point to experience everything worth doing when it comes to cultural endeavors."

"So you know what a rich voice he has?"

"I do."

He didn't. Paying the kind of money it would take to see someone as well-known and appreciated as Mr. Hastings was out of the question. But his plan had worked and Mrs. Giles was no longer making her daughter uncomfortable. In fact, after Mrs. Giles extolled the virtues of Mr. Hastings' voice, she went on to talk about other fine singers she'd heard in the past. He couldn't be sure, but he thought Miss Giles appreciated his efforts, if he judged her smile correctly. And he was glad he could make the afternoon enjoyable for her.

Chapter Six

"Regina, Lord Pennella is in the drawing room," her lady's maid said the next day.

From her bedchamber window, Regina glanced up from the book she was reading. "I'll be down in a moment."

Her lady's maid offered a nod and shut the door. She put her book aside and rose to her feet. She went to the mirror and checked her reflection, just as she had the day before when Lord Davenport visited. As Lady Seyton suggested, she wore a dress that showed a hint of her cleavage. It was a ridiculous thing to aim for, but Lady Seyton insisted it was to get the gentleman to think about marriage.

"A lady who is suitable for marriage does well to remind the potential husband that he'll have fun trying for the heir if he chooses her," Lady Seyton had said.

Even now, Regina had to fight the urge to roll her eyes. The little she had gathered in her lessons boiled down to the gentleman's need for praise and lovemaking. That was about it. How Lady Seyton considered this worthy of money, Regina could only guess. But she had an impressive history of success with her patrons, so she couldn't argue with her record. It just seemed foolish that the lessons took a couple weeks.

With a sigh, she left her bedchamber. She told herself this was just another gentleman her mother wished to snare on her behalf. Each of these encounters required a great deal of her, and after yesterday, she was already tired. Though, she had enjoyed Lord Davenport's visit. He had a way of handling her mother that impressed her. None of the other gentlemen had known how to respond to her. Indeed, most of them humored her and played along. She wondered if Lord Pennella would be the same or if he'd be able to take a kind, but firm, stand against her mother's desire to gossip. If nothing else, Regina was looking forward to finding out.

She arrived in the drawing room before Lord Pennella noticed her. He was handsome enough, she supposed. A bit more on the muscular side than she preferred, though she liked the broad shoulders. Hair a bit lighter than Lord Davenport's but still brown. At the moment, he was examining his reflection in the window. Her eyebrows rose in interest. None of the gentlemen who'd come by had done something like that before.

He smoothed his hair then winked at himself. And it was at that point she knew he was not the kind of person she wanted to spend the afternoon with, much less the rest of her life. Thank goodness he wasn't the only gentleman who had a title in London or else she'd have to run off before her mother could chain her to him.

Clearing her throat to get his attention, she curtsied. "Lord Pennella, forgive me for taking so long to come down."

Though it was to her benefit she did. She'd do well to do that in the future with the others who came by. Watching a gentleman who didn't know he was being watched was surprisingly enlightening.

He approached her and bowed. "It was well worth the wait, Miss Giles. You're even lovelier than the first time I met you."

Resisting the urge to gag, she managed to smile. Did he really believe she wouldn't see through the lie? "Thank you, my lord."

The butler brought in the tray with tea, and she invited Lord Pennella to sit and have a drink with her. It was the same old familiar routine, one that Lady Seyton insisted would establish a rapport with the gentleman in question. That was why her mother demanded Regina spend a few minutes in the drawing room alone with each potential suitor.

Regina sat in her usual spot and poured tea in both of their cups, but on this day, she decided she'd rather not allow the gentleman a generous view of her cleavage. Instead, she chose an angle that offered him a better view of her shoulder. She saw no reason to encourage him.

"Do you come to London often?" she asked.

"From time to time when I've tired of my many travels to other countries," he replied.

Her eyebrows rose. "Oh?"

"Yes. I find it expands my world and gives me a better perspective on life. I meet fascinating new people and explore the different cultures the world has to offer."

She couldn't fault him for that. A good dose of curiosity was a healthy thing. If she hadn't caught him winking at himself, she might be intrigued to learn more about him.

"How about you?" he asked as he accepted the cup she offered. "Do you travel?"

"I'm afraid with all the social engagements my mother requires me to attend, I'm not allowed the luxury of travel," she replied then sipped her tea.

"Well, there's nothing wrong with social engagements. I go to many of them myself."

"I didn't say there was anything wrong with it. I'm just explaining why we don't travel often."

"But you have traveled?"

"A few times in the past. France, Italy, Greece."

"Those are good countries."

She nodded. "I enjoyed them."

"So you have been outside of England and tasted a piece of the world." He smiled at her in a way that made her feel like a young child who was to be patted on the head for such a good deed. "It's refreshing to meet a young lady who has some life experience."

Yes, indeed she had plenty of experience if one considered visiting the stores in those countries with a mother who was searching for something "new" and "different" to wear. But she chose to keep quiet about this little secret.

"Tell me," he began after he drank some tea, "have you been in London all Season?"

"Yes."

"But you haven't been to many of the balls, have you?"

"I've been to most of them." Where was he going with this?

"That's strange."

"What's strange?"

He shrugged, though he shot her what was probably the same smile he gave every lady he hoped to charm. "You're so beautiful. I should have noticed you sooner."

"Perhaps there were ladies at the other balls who were more beautiful than me and that's why I didn't catch your attention sooner," she suggested, intentionally putting him on the spot and wondering what he'd do about it.

As it turned out, his face grew pink.

Her mother entered the drawing room, relieving him of having to come up with an adequate response. "Lord Pennella, I presume?" her mother greeted.

He set the cup on the tray and bowed to her. "At your service, Mrs. Giles. I was just enjoying a pleasant chat with your charming and lovely daughter."

Charming and lovely? Regina highly doubted the sincerity in his words. But to give him the benefit of the doubt, she reasoned he was merely being polite.

"Thank you, my lord," her mother replied, glancing her way in obvious pleasure.

Regina forced a smile in return then quickly looked down at her hands so she wouldn't have to maintain eye contact with her. Yesterday hadn't been so awkward. In fact, it'd been very nice. She wondered if Lord Davenport would ask to see her again.

"Regina, are you ready to go to the museum?" her mother called out.

Unaware that her mother and Lord Pennella had been speaking, Regina turned her attention back to them. With a nod, she went over to them. "Yes, I'm ready."

Regina joined them in Lord Pennella's carriage, and her mother made a show of fussing over how expensive it must have been.

"We wanted an interior so fine but couldn't afford such lavish upholstery," her mother rambled as she ran her hand along the edge of the seat.

"You only live once," Lord Pennella said with a laugh. "I see no reason to deny the very best when I escort beautiful ladies around town."

Her mother chuckled, and Regina turned her gaze to the window. Fortunately, her mother wasn't paying attention to her or else she'd never hear the end of it.

"Of course, I hear Lord Edon also has a fine carriage," her mother spoke up.

Regina grimaced. Her mother was trying to gather information from him, just as she'd tried it with Lord Davenport and the other gentlemen they'd been out with that Season.

"It's no secret that Lord Edon has the best carriage in all of London," Lord Pennella said. "He keeps winning every single game he ever plays."

"Does he?" Her mother's eyebrows rose in interest. "I heard he was lucky."

"Lucky?" He laughed and shook his head. "No, he's not just lucky. He's ruthless. He claims that he doesn't want to win every game, but that's what he does. Thankfully, his father-in-law put an end to it or else I'd have no money left."

Her mother laughed at his joke. "I bet you're better off not gambling, my lord."

"Perhaps I would be, but I have to admit that there's a certain thrill in it. The chance of winning or losing is a powerful one. It's the risk, and the bigger the risk, the greater the thrill."

Regina glanced at him. He seemed particularly pleased with himself, and it only affirmed her initial thought about him. He was already in love...with himself.

The carriage came to a stop at the museum. With a sigh, Regina followed them out of the carriage, bracing herself for the mindless chatter she'd likely have to suffer through for the next couple hours. No doubt, it was going to be a long and exhausting afternoon.

A FIRM HAND CLASPED Toby's shoulder. Toby glanced up from the paper he was reading at White's. He'd hoped that since Pennella was supposed to be at the museum with Miss Giles and her mother, it would afford him some peace.

But here Pennella was, and he'd brought the self-satisfied smirk with him. "The bet is as good as settled," he said as he sat across from Toby. He crossed his legs and clasped his hands over his lap. "So, when would you like to hand me your estate?"

"Miss Giles accepted your proposal?" Toby asked, trying not to give away his apprehension.

"I haven't proposed yet."

Toby relaxed. Good. That meant he still had a chance. "Then you're a little premature."

He shrugged. "The proposal is a mere formality. We all knew I had a better chance of winning, and today only sealed the deal."

"How so?"

"I have a gift for keeping ladies enraptured."

Ignoring the few gentlemen who stopped their talk to listen to them, Toby forced out, "And how did you enrapture them?"

"Not them. Her."

"Her?"

"The mother. Mrs. Giles. I regaled her with all sorts of amusing anecdotes."

"Did you?"

"Yes. Her mother was curious about a lot of the nobility, so I let her in on some little tidbits of information she won't find in the scandal sheets. You know, the way to a lady is through her mother. If you can win her mother over, then the battle's already won."

For the first time since he'd made the wager with Pennella, Toby felt a spark of hope. Maybe he had a chance with Regina after all. Pennella could delude himself all he wanted. In fact, the more he did, the better. "Until Miss Giles accepts your proposal, the wager stands." He rose to his feet. "I think I'll offer Miss Giles my condolences. The poor thing must be distraught after spending the afternoon with you."

The other gentlemen chuckled, but Pennella narrowed his eyes at him. If Pennella had taken the time to listen to Miss Giles, he would have realized she didn't like gossip. But he didn't, and that gave Toby a surprising advantage. And this was one advantage he was going to pursue.

Going to her house unannounced would never do, but he could send her a request for another visit. By the time he reached his townhouse, he knew exactly how he'd word the calling card. And he didn't waste any time in sending it out.

Chapter Seven

"You received a second request from Lord Davenport to see you?" Lady Seyton asked two days later as Regina and her mother sat in Lady Seyton's drawing room.

Though Lady Seyton had directed the question to Regina, her mother spoke on her behalf. "Yes, we did."

We? Regina bit her lower lip so she wouldn't say something. There was no 'we' in the calling card he sent. It was only for her. But leave it to her mother to treat this as if they were both being courted.

Lady Seyton chuckled as she poured them a cup of tea. "The first time together is always the hardest one. A second request from the gentleman almost assures a proposal is imminent."

Regina's mother let out a squeal of delight. "I just knew it!" She squeezed Regina's arm before Regina could take her cup of tea. "I just knew he was interested in you."

"You think all gentlemen are interested in me," Regina reminded her then took the cup from Lady Seyton.

"But this one wants to see you again. It's a good sign."

"I agree with your mother," Lady Seyton said then sipped her tea. "This just might be the one."

As much as the prospect excited her, Regina couldn't help but think it was too soon. The walk in the park was very enjoyable, more so than she thought possible. But it was only one time. What if the second venture didn't go so well?

What a silly question. Regina knew what it meant. It meant she had to start all over again, something she dreaded. Not only had she found

Lord Davenport refreshing, but she didn't know if she had the strength to go through the initial pleasantries with someone else. All right. Perhaps she hadn't been so pleasant with Lord Davenport, but he'd had a surprisingly good sense of humor about the whole thing. It was hard not to find such a gentleman attractive. More than just attractive, really. He was someone she could fall in love with.

After they finished the tea, her mother patted Regina on the arm and looked at Lady Seyton. "Now that we have a gentleman who wants another visit, what is the best way to proceed?"

"I'd say it's a good idea to keep doing what you've been doing all along," Lady Seyton replied. "Obviously, it works."

"But surely, there must be something more to it than that," her mother pressed.

"Besides delighting him with your personality, I can't think of much more a titled gentleman wants except to get an heir."

Her mother glanced Regina's way, and Regina shrugged. Why Lord Davenport liked her well enough to want to see her again, she didn't know. She'd been pretty skeptical about gentlemen and marriage in particular. The fact that she hadn't scared him off spoke volumes of how much the poor man could endure, something that probably amazed her mother to no end.

Her mother offered her a smile. "Perhaps we ought to remind him of how important heirs are to gentlemen. I'll hint about such things when he comes by."

Regina's eyes grew wide. Good heavens! Did her mother really think that was a good idea?

"That's a good idea," Lady Seyton replied. "It never hurts for someone other than the lady to subtly remind him of these things."

"I can certainly do it, and I assure you I'll choose my words with great care." Her mother stood up. "Thank you for your advice, my lady."

Lady Seyton rose to her feet, Regina quickly following. "I fully expect this is the one who'll propose."

Her mother's smile widened at the prospect, and Regina had to admit she hoped Lady Seyton was right.

ON THE DAY LORD DAVENPORT was due to arrive, Regina had planned to wait in her bedchamber for his arrival, but the task proved much too daunting. She tried to focus on her book. After her tenth failed attempt to understand what she was reading, she gave up and put the book aside.

Not sure what to do with her time until he arrived, she left her bedchamber and slowly walked down the hall. To her surprise, her mother came rushing up the stairs.

"Are you sure it's appropriate for a lady to be caught running through the house?" Regina asked, a hint of amusement in her tone.

"I have good reason to run," her mother insisted and took her by the arm before guiding her back to her bedchamber.

"What's wrong? Is my hair out of place or my dress not properly secure?"

"No, no. Nothing like that." Once they were in her bedchamber, her mother shut the door and turned to her, a wide smile on her face. She took a calling card out of her pocket and showed it to her. "Lord Pennella wants to see you again, too."

"What?"

"Isn't it wonderful? You have your pick of two titled gentlemen."

Regina could hardly speak. She thought for sure Lord Pennella wouldn't want to see her again after the way she talked to him.

"I'm going to give a little extra money to Lady Seyton. Her techniques work like a charm," her mother added. "I'll send Lord Pennella a card back and accept on your behalf."

Regina opened her mouth to stop her, but her mother hurried out of the room. She considered calling after her mother. But really, what good would it do? Her mother would love to tell her friends that her daughter had two titled gentlemen vying for her hand. The least Regina could do was give her mother the luxury of doing that. It wasn't like she had to say yes if Lord Pennella proposed.

"Miss Giles," her lady's maid said, peering into the bedchamber, "Lord Davenport is here."

Good. A much needed distraction. Right now, she would enjoy the afternoon. She thanked her lady's maid then went down the stairs. Recalling the way Lord Pennella had admired his reflection in the window, she kept her steps silent as she approached the drawing room.

She stopped before she reached the open door, so he wouldn't see her. She peeked into the room. Lord Davenport stood by the window, just as Lord Pennella had. But he had his hat in his hands and his gaze was focused on the floor.

"I hope you'll be at Lord Toplyn's ball." He shook his head. "No, that doesn't work." He paused. "I was planning on going to Lord Toplyn's ball and wondered if you'll be there." He sighed and tapped the hat.

It took her a moment to realize he was trying to think of a way to ask if he could see her again. He probably didn't want to seem too eager. The thought made her skin warm in pleasure. It was very sweet that he worried so much over whether or not he could spend time with her. Indeed, it was a refreshing change from the other gentlemen she'd met. Lord Davenport really was sincere in his affections for her.

He turned to the window and hesitated a few seconds then asked, "Did you hear Lord Toplyn's having a ball?" Seeming to be satisfied, he nodded and looked toward the doorway.

She took that as her cue. After she entered the room, she curtsied. "Good afternoon, my lord."

He bowed. "It's an honor to be here."

"The butler will bring our tea in soon. Will you have a seat?"

He nodded and sat on the settee.

She hesitated to sit by him. If he'd been Lord Pennella, she wouldn't have even considered it. But this was Lord Davenport, and she wanted to. In a bold move that she never thought she'd take, she sat next to him and noted that he smiled. Relaxing since he hadn't been taken aback by her bold move, she returned his smile and asked, "How have you been since we last talked?"

"Good. And you?"

"I've been fine. Nothing of interest happened."

"It didn't?"

She shook her head. She hadn't realized how much she'd been looking forward to seeing him again until that moment. "No, it didn't. I'm glad you came by today."

"You are?"

She studied his expression and fought the urge to chuckle. If she guessed right, he worried that she hadn't given him a second thought over the past three days. "Yes, I am."

The butler came in and set the tray of tea in front of them.

She waited until he left before she continued talking. "I know it doesn't seem like I enjoy much about London," she began as she poured his tea.

"Oh, I wouldn't say that," he quickly spoke up. "You seemed to enjoy the park the other day."

"Yes, I did. And I wanted to thank you for steering my mother away from gossip. It was nice to spend an afternoon without listening to who is doing what and who performed the worst scandal." She handed him his cup and poured tea into hers. "Maybe if I didn't have to listen to it so much, I wouldn't mind."

"I don't think the people involved in the scandal want others talking about it." He cleared his throat. "I know I wouldn't."

"I doubt my mother would either. It's different when you're the one on display." She put the teapot down and returned his smile.

"I agree. And sometimes a person stumbles into a situation without even meaning to."

"Exactly. We don't know why the person did what they did. It's not up to us to judge their motives."

After a moment, he sipped his tea. "I was wondering, did you hear Lord Toplyn's having a ball?"

Hiding her smile, she nodded. "My mother mentioned it. She makes it a point to go to as many as she can."

"Well, I'll be there, and I'd be honored if you saved two dances for me."

Pleased, her face grew warm. "I'll do that."

She couldn't recall a time when anyone had such a pleasant effect on her. It was more than the beginning of romantic attraction that she felt. Deep down, she knew this was a gentleman who had the potential to be a friend, a companion she could spend her life with, sharing its ups and downs. Perhaps he sensed the same connection she did.

"Lord Davenport," her mother said, breezing into the room, "it's good to see you again."

She gave an elaborate curtsy that almost made Regina spit out her tea. But she managed to swallow it before any damage was done.

Lord Davenport quickly set his cup down and bowed. "Thanks for having me."

"Oh, anytime," her mother replied. She sat in the chair close to Regina and gestured for Lord Davenport to sit. "I thought we'd sit and talk for a while before going out."

Sensing her mother was up to something, Regina studied her expression.

"In fact," her mother began as she took Regina's cup from her and added more tea to it, "just last night, my daughter and I were talking."

Regina's eyes narrowed as her mother added a lump of sugar to the tea and stirred it with a spoon. "Where are you going with this?" Regina asked, sure she didn't want to know. Morbid curiosity, however, was getting the best of her.

"You needn't be so shy about it," her mother told her then handed her the cup. "Drink up, dear."

Regina shook her head and handed it back to her. "I'm not thirsty anymore. You take it."

"Very well." Her mother took a sip. "It's very good. I should pay my compliments to Cook."

"It is good tea," Lord Davenport said.

"Would you like more?" her mother offered.

"No, thank you. Like your daughter, I've had enough," he replied.

Regina wondered why her mother was stalling. There was obviously something on her mind—something she was scheming—and she had yet to come out and say what it was. And worse, the longer she waited, the more uncomfortable Regina felt.

"We usually drink green tea," her mother rambled. "It's supposed to be good for your health. Or so I've heard. But lately, we've been trying different flavors. Sometimes you have to do that, you know. Do something different so you can find out what you might be missing."

"Where are you going with this, Mother?" Regina asked again. If she had any clue, she could take measures to turn the conversation in another direction.

"Just talking about tea."

No, she was only using that as a means to get to what she really wanted to discuss. Regina closed her eyes for a moment and prayed for patience.

"As I was saying," her mother continued, "trying something new might be exciting."

"Are you referring to traveling?" Lord Davenport asked, his eyebrows furrowed.

"No, though that is a good way of seeing what else life has to offer," her mother said. "There's more to the world than the little corner we live in." Before Regina could open her mouth and suggest her mother get on with it, her mother gave the tea back to her. "What do you think of this black tea, dear? It's good, isn't it? Drink up."

Deciding she'd had enough of this silly game, Regina put the cup back on the table. "This isn't about tea, and I know it. What are you getting at?"

"Children. Specifically, grandchildren for me in my old age," her mother blurted out.

Regina's jaw dropped. They had no such conversation!

"Lord Davenport," her mother continued, "I assure you that my daughter would make a wonderful mother. She comes from a healthy stock, too. She could have many sons."

"That's enough, Mother," she spoke up once she could talk. She stood up. "Now is a good time to go to the carriage."

Fortunately, Lord Davenport rose to his feet and agreed that a carriage ride sounded like a good idea. Relieved, she accepted his arm and hurried out of the room, leaving her mother behind them to catch up.

Chapter Eight

"You're not still upset with me, are you?" Regina's mother asked the next morning during breakfast.

Regina glanced at her father who was buttering his biscuit. Why didn't he ever take measures to restrain her mother's tongue in the twenty-three years of their marriage?

"Regina?" her mother pressed, leaning toward her. "Are you really going to ignore me?"

Regina set the fork next to the fruit on her plate and sighed. "Are you not aware the butler's in the room?" she whispered.

Her mother looked over her shoulder. "Harold, will you please leave us for a few moments?"

The butler left the room and closed the door to ensure their privacy.

"Now, will you please talk to me?" her mother asked, turning back to her.

"Fine," Regina finally relented. "You want me to tell you the truth? The truth is you embarrassed me yesterday."

Her mother's eyes grew wide, and she glanced at her father who shrugged. "Regina, the last thing I want to do is embarrass you."

"Then in the future, don't tell any gentleman who comes to see me that you want grandchildren."

Her father nearly choked on the biscuit he'd just put in his mouth.

"You see?" Regina motioned to him. "Even he knows such talk is inappropriate."

"Inappropriate?" Her mother had the audacity to appear surprised. "Lady Seyton told me to do it."

"She did no such thing."

"She said we should get the gentlemen to think of having an heir."

"I'm sure she meant to be subtle about it."

"There was nothing wrong with the way I brought up the subject."

"You practically offered my services as a brood mare."

Her mother gasped and pressed her hand to her chest. "I did no such thing."

Glancing at her father, Regina said, "She said I came from good stock and could give him many sons."

Her father winced. "That was a little too bold, my dear," he told her mother.

"Well, gentlemen aren't known for taking hints. They require boldness," her mother insisted. "I recall having to tell you it was time for you to get married since you were in your late thirties."

"That was different," he said. "The gentlemen coming to see Regina want to get married. There's no need to convince them."

"But they need to be convinced that they're better off marrying her," she gestured to Regina, "than someone else."

Regina almost said she already knew which gentleman she wanted to marry but held her tongue. Who knew what her mother would do with such information?

"Camilla, you know I don't often come down on you about these things," her father gently said. "But in this case, I must insist you refrain from saying such things in the future."

With a sigh, her mother nodded. "Fine. I won't speak of children or grandchildren anymore."

"Thank you, Father," Regina told him.

"Why are you thanking him?" her mother asked. "I'm the one who promised not to do it."

When Regina looked heavenward, her father chuckled. "Why don't you two go shopping?"

"What a lovely idea!" Standing up from her half-eaten meal, her mother gestured to Regina. "I saw the most beautiful gold dress the other day. It's absolutely divine. It'll be perfect for Lord Toplyn's ball."

Regina's ears perked up. Lord Davenport would be at the ball. Without bothering to finish her own meal, she jumped up and followed her mother out of the room.

A LOUD CHEER ROSE FROM the gaming room at White's as Toby walked through the front door. Catching Orlando lounging by the window, he went over to him. "What's the big commotion in the other room?"

Orlando forced his gaze off the window so he could look at him. "They're betting on which one of you will get two dances with Miss Giles at Lord Toplyn's ball."

Feeling a smile tugging at his lips, he sat by his friend and leaned toward him. "That's an easy one. I will."

Orlando's eyebrow arched. "You're not so easily given to bragging. That's Pennella's thing."

"It's not bragging if it's the truth. I went to see her yesterday, and she promised she'd save two dances for me." In a lower voice, he added, "She's really a marvelous lady. She's witty, intelligent, and funny. It seems a shame that I hadn't met her sooner."

"I don't believe it," Orlando said as he straightened in his seat.

"Don't believe what?"

"You love her."

"I don't know. It's a little too soon for love." Even as he voiced the protest, his heartbeat picked up in excitement. "But I think you're right."

"You should worry about falling in love with someone who was only supposed to be a bet. What if she chooses Pennella?"

"She won't."

"How can you be sure?"

"Because we get along as if we've known each other our entire lives. I never met anyone like her before."

Orlando shook his head. "I'm not sure it's a good idea to fall in love with her."

"It's perfect. This way when she chooses me, I won't have to quietly end things with her. I can really go through with it and marry her."

"And take Pennella's estate?"

Toby blinked. He'd forgotten that part of the wager. And the reminder made him hesitate. Pennella always had the best carriage, clothes, and townhouse. He probably had a good fortune to his name. If Toby did acquire it, he wouldn't have to come into the marriage with Miss Giles with only a title and a rundown country estate.

Orlando shook his head. "Unbelievable."

"No, I won't take his estate," Toby relented. Orlando was right. Going that far would be cruel. All Toby had wanted when this whole thing began was to wipe the smirk off of Pennella's face and do right by the lady. "I won't take his estate. I'll play some cards with him and lose the hand so he gets it back. That way, he'll think he won it back, fair and square."

"While I know Pennella would be thrilled to take everything you have-"

"Which is nothing," Toby interjected.

Orlando shot him an amused look. "My point is that Pennella has no conscience about such things, but you're better than that."

"Yes, I know." Lucky him, Toby thought with a hint of sarcasm.

"I wouldn't be friends with you if you were like him."

Toby couldn't recall a time when he heard his friend pay him a higher compliment. "Thank you."

The gentlemen adjourned from the other room, and Toplyn headed in their direction. Surprised, Toby straightened in his seat.

Toplyn pulled up a chair and sat next to him. "Have you heard how high the bet is between you and Pennella?"

Toby glanced at Orlando, not sure he wanted to know but finding himself intrigued. "No. What is today's amount?"

"One hundred pounds that you'll secure two dances with Miss Giles and a thousand on whether or not you'll win her hand," Toplyn said. "I bet my money on you."

"Why would you do something foolish like that?" Orlando asked.

Toby shot his friend a pointed look. Did he secretly believe Pennella was going to win?

"Sorry." Orlando shrugged. "I think the whole bet is outrageous."

"Though you encouraged it the other day?" Toby asked.

"Only to get everyone's attention off the fight you and Pennella were having."

"So you think this whole thing is ridiculous after all?"

"Of course, I do."

"You and Roderick," Toplyn replied with a sigh. "Even Edon won't place a bet." In a lower voice, he added, "And I used to bet on everything he did because I was sure to win. I miss the days when he bet on everything he could."

"So," Orlando began, "what you're saying is that your days of riding on his coattails are over?"

"I wouldn't say I was riding his coattails," Toplyn replied. "But his knack for winning every time did help me amass the wealth my father squandered."

Toby wished he had thought to bet on things that Edon did. If he had, he'd probably be in better financial shape, too.

Orlando shifted in his chair. "You better be careful. Now that you have to place bets without his help, you might lose everything you gained."

"Oh, this is the last bet I'm making, and I have a feeling I'll win." Toplyn gave Toby a wink. "I happen to know Miss Giles' father."

At this announcement, Toby smiled and glanced at Orlando whose eyes grew wide. Unable to resist asking the question, Toby turned his attention back to Toplyn. "What did her father tell you?"

"Nothing in so many words. He just said that he believes his daughter looks forward to seeing you again. She has expressed no such sentiment for Pennella."

If that didn't seal it, then nothing would. Toby had suspected Miss Giles reciprocated his feelings, and it delighted him to no end to know she did for sure. He experienced a newfound confidence he hadn't felt in a long time.

Toplyn patted him on the shoulder then stood up. "You're the first person who has put Pennella in his place."

As the gentleman left, Toby shot Orlando a wide smile, but Orlando warned, "Don't let this go to your head."

"You have nothing to worry about," Toby assured him. "The last thing I want to do is be like Pennella. I just want to marry Miss Giles and live happily ever after."

"You better hope she doesn't find out about the wager."

"She won't."

"For your sake, I hope not."

Toby shook his head. "I didn't take you for a pessimist."

"I'm not, but if word of this wager reaches Miss Giles, she might not marry you."

"I'm not going to tell her, if that's what you think. I know better than that. I doubt Pennella would say anything."

"I know you and Pennella wouldn't tell her."

Toby frowned. "You plan to?"

"Of course not. I wouldn't do that, but someone might find out and tell her."

"The only people who know are here at White's, and what happens here, stays here."

"I hope you're right." Orlando stood up. "You want to play some cards?"

With a nod, Toby followed him to a card table. Orlando's worries were for nothing. He was sure of it.

REGINA STIFLED A YAWN as Lord Pennella rambled on about a bullfight he'd watched while in Spain. Her mother, however, was enraptured with his every word. The two of them got along much better than she and Lord Pennella did. But if her mother thought she was going to marry Lord Pennella simply because her mother wished it, she had another thing coming. Fortunately, Lord Pennella wasn't the only one who was coming by to see her. She had Lord Davenport's attention as well.

Just thinking of seeing him that evening made her pulse race with excitement. It seemed like a long time since she'd seen him, but it had only been the other day. Was this what love felt like? The quickened heartbeat whenever that someone was near? The warmth in the face at the mere thought of his name? She'd never been in love before. And she had assumed such a feeling wouldn't factor into her marriage. But it looked like she just might be one of the fortunate few who would get to have a love match.

Her mother let out a shrill cackle that made her wince. She knew her mother didn't intend for her laughter to come out that way, but when she was excited enough, that's what happened.

"Surely, you jest," her mother said, waving her hand dismissively at him.

"I assure you, I'm not," Lord Pennella told her then sipped his tea. He settled the cup back in the saucer and gave Regina a wink. "Bulls can be rather defiant creatures when they don't get their way, and that matador wasn't about to let it win. He hung onto the bull's horns and didn't let go."

Her mother laughed again.

Regina had never heard of anything so ridiculous. She didn't believe for a moment a man could actually do that without risking serious injury—or worse. If Lord Pennella expected her to believe this particular fighter could stand on a bull's back and hold onto its horns without getting thrown off, he misjudged just how cynical she could be. What she suspected he was doing was embellishing the story for her mother's sake. The more dramatic the tale, the more her mother loved it.

Her mother glanced her way, and by the silent message in her eyes, Regina knew she better laugh at whatever 'witty' thing Lord Pennella was saying or she'd get a lecture on how rude she'd been. Regina forced out a laugh, hoping it was convincing enough for her mother. By the way her mother relaxed, she was assured it was.

"Well, now that I've told the story about the best bullfight I'd ever seen," he said as he grabbed the last tart, "I thought you'd like to see the gardens at my friend's estate. The flowers are absolutely gorgeous this time of year, and being two beautiful ladies, I know you appreciate beauty." He bit into the tart and shot her another wink.

Regina resisted the urge to roll her eyes. He was much too obvious. Why couldn't her mother see how deceptive he was? He was clearly up to something. Regina could spot that a mile away.

"It sounds lovely," her mother said, nodding with all the enthusiasm of a young girl in love.

Good heavens! Granted, her mother wasn't really infatuated with him, but she was in love with the idea of Regina marrying him. Her gut tightened. If Lord Davenport didn't propose soon, her mother might somehow figure out a way to get her to marry Lord Pennella instead. She knew Lord Davenport was interested in her, but was he interested enough to marry her?

She bit her lower lip. That was the real question. She suspected he was. He looked at her in a way that no one else—not even Lord Pennella—did. There was a tenderness in his gaze that made her weak in the knees. But he wasn't the charmer that Lord Pennella was.

Her mother rose to her feet and gestured for Regina to do the same. "We'd be delighted to spend the afternoon with you. I, for one, can't recall a time when I've had such a delightful visit. You tell the most fascinating stories."

"All true, I assure you," he said after he finished the last of the tart. He wiped his fingers on the napkin and set it back on the tray. He rose to his feet and extended one arm to Regina and the other to her mother. "I am fortunate to have two lovely ladies spend the afternoon with me. All the gentlemen will be envious."

Her mother giggled. "You flatter us too much, my lord." She paused and added, "Don't stop."

He laughed and assured her he wouldn't.

How Regina wished her mother would stop encouraging him! She couldn't fight the nagging suspicion that if she didn't do something drastic, she was going to spend the rest of her life being subjected to wild tales and endless gossip.

This evening at the ball was her best chance. She was going to have to find out if Lord Davenport intended to propose to her. As much as she hated to do it, she didn't see what other choice she had. Yes. She'd talk to him tonight.

Chapter Nine

Regina picked up her fan and waved it. She was hot. Sweat trickled down her back, something she'd rather not think about when she wore an expensive gown. The ball was a success. People were enjoying themselves immensely, and laughter swirled around her as her gaze kept sweeping the room in hopes she'd see Lord Davenport. He said he'd be here, and she had no doubt he would be. But she hoped he would come before Lord Pennella did.

When she finally saw him enter the ballroom, her heart skipped a beat. There was no denying it. She was in love with him. Maybe their time together had been short, but she couldn't resist the way he made her skin tingle with pleasure at the mere sight of him.

Excited, she turned to her mother who was talking to Lady Seyton about the gowns the ladies were wearing.

"My Regina seems better dressed than over half the room," her mother bragged.

"To be fair," Lady Seyton replied, "not all have a father who is as well off as your husband."

"I suppose you're right." Her mother let out a long sigh. "It's a shame that my husband has no title. He has more money than some of the titled gentlemen here, I bet."

"Oh, indeed. That could work to your daughter's benefit if she wished. Marriages made for money and titles happen all the time. It's part of what makes the marriage mart so interesting to watch."

Her mother chuckled. "I would have to agree with your astute observation."

"Mother," Regina said.

"Yes, Regina?" Her mother turned to look at her.

"Lord Davenport requested a dance with me earlier today." In fact, he had asked for two, something that delighted her the more she thought about it.

Her mother scanned the room. "Isn't Lord Pennella here? I want you to dance with him."

"He's not here yet," Regina replied, already knowing a big fight was coming over who she'd be marrying. There was no way her mother was going to give her blessing to Lord Davenport when Lord Pennella appeared to be interested as well. Releasing her breath, she added, "It's only a dance, Mother."

Her mother finally nodded. "You're right. But I do hope you'll save a dance or two for Lord Pennella."

If that was what it was going to take, then so be it. "I will."

Her mother relaxed but added, "Don't get too attached yet. You still have options."

Lord Davenport approached, and Regina turned her attention to him. He looked more and more handsome each time she saw him. Maybe he wasn't as striking as Lord Pennella, but he was definitely attractive in his own right. "Good evening, Miss Giles," he greeted with a bow. "Mrs. Giles, Lady Seyton."

After they curtsied, he asked Regina to dance with him. Though her mother smiled, she didn't give him the same glowing smile she gave Lord Pennella. Regina took his arm and went to where the couples waited for the orchestra to start the music. She didn't know how she was going to politely bring up the topic of a proposal. The idea sounded much easier when she wasn't right in front of him.

When the music began, he led her in the dance. "You look beautiful," he told her.

"Thank you."

As she turned, she saw Lord Pennella enter the room. His gaze went to her and Lord Davenport, and she caught a flicker of something in his eyes. Jealousy perhaps? That almost seemed absurd. She got the feeling he didn't really care for her. He seemed much too enamored with himself. But there was no denying the fact that he wasn't happy to see her with Lord Davenport. Not that it was any of his concern. She had a right to be with whoever she wanted.

"I'm glad you came," Lord Davenport said, bringing her attention back to him.

"I said I would be here."

"Yes, but anything could have prevented you from coming."

"No, nothing could have stopped me from coming. I wanted to see you."

His smile widened, and she knew she'd said the right thing. "I wanted to see you, too. In fact, I was hoping to see you again. Maybe tomorrow, if you're not otherwise engaged?"

Since he mentioned seeing her so soon, she took that as a good sign. "I'd like that. I enjoy our times together."

"I do, too," he softly said.

Her heart leapt at the way he said those words. Yes, they would have a love match, something envied by many who had to marry for other reasons. "My lord, forgive me if I'm too bold in my speech, but I do hope that I will get to see more of you in the future."

"I would like nothing more."

That was a promising sign. She tried to think of a way to mention a proposal, but the music came to an end. The whole thing happened much too fast. If it hadn't been for the uncertainty of what to say, she would have gotten more in. But there was one more dance she could have with him, and maybe in that one, she wouldn't hesitate to say what was really on her mind.

"It was a pleasure, Miss Giles," he said and squeezed her hand. "I'll dance with you in a bit. It looks like my friend needs to talk to me."

She followed his gaze and saw a gentleman waving at him from across the room.

"That's Lord Reddington," he said. "You'll get better acquainted with him in the future."

Pleased since it implied there could very well be a proposal, she said, "I look forward to it."

"I'll miss you until the next dance."

The way he looked at her, as if he thought she was the most important lady in the room, made her face warm with pleasure. "I will miss you, too, my lord."

"Toby," he whispered.

His name! He'd given her his name. Yes, he was thinking along the lines of a proposal. She just knew it!

She watched as Toby and Lord Reddington headed down one of the hallways, her smile growing wider. When she danced with him again, she'd ask him if he could talk to her father about marrying her. If he did it before Lord Pennella, then her mother would have a harder time convincing her father to accept Lord Pennella's offer.

She headed back to her mother but didn't find her right away. After searching a little more, she found that her mother was talking to Lord Pennella. She edged her way along several groups of people so her mother and Lord Pennella wouldn't see her. Opening her fan, she covered her face and came up behind them, hoping her mother wouldn't look over her shoulder.

At the moment, her mother was laughing at whatever ridiculous thing he was saying.

"I do so delight in your stories, my lord," her mother gushed.

"Well, I delight in telling them," he quipped.

She laughed again and waved her hand at him. "You are much too amusing. I shall swoon from so much laughter."

"If you do, I'll catch you."

This set her into another round of giggles, and Regina had to bite back the urge to tell her mother to stop it. She was making a fool of herself by falling all over Lord Pennella. The gentleman truly wasn't worth it.

"I have a confession to make," her mother told him in a lower voice.

"A confession? Sounds like a juicy tidbit. Do you know how Lady Edon tamed her husband?"

"No. That is something I don't think any of us will ever figure out. What I wish to say is that I'd like for you to be my son-in-law."

"In that case, I'll share a confidence with you. I'd like nothing more than to be your son-in-law."

"Excellent. Then we are of the same mind."

He nodded.

"Regina's father will have the final say in who she marries. Regina thinks she does, but the truth is, he is the one who will make the decision."

Regina had been under no such delusion that if two gentlemen were vying for her hand that she'd get to decide which one she'd marry. She just hadn't believed she'd have two to choose from.

"You have a suggestion on how I might secure a betrothal?" Lord Pennella asked her mother, his voice hinting that he hoped she would tell him the secret.

"I do," she replied. "My husband is a businessman. And a shrewd one at that. What he most appreciates is making new acquaintances that can lead to profitable ventures. Do you happen to know anyone who might meet that requirement?"

Regina gritted her teeth. She didn't like the way this was going. If her father benefited from knowing Lord Pennella in such a way, there was no chance Toby could talk her father into letting him marry her.

"My dear," her mother said, startled, "I didn't see you standing there."

Regina looked over at her mother and lowered her fan. "Oh, I didn't want to interrupt your conversation," she quickly fibbed and waved the fan. She didn't think it was possible, but she was even hotter than before.

"What a thoughtful child," her mother replied. "She learned very well when we taught her to wait until she is talked to before speaking. Good manners are important for a countess."

"That is true," Lord Pennella said and smiled at her. "It's always good when a lady is thoughtful in her conduct."

Regina forced a smile in return. As much as she wanted to find Toby, she couldn't very well slip off down the hallway right now. At the moment, she was trapped, but at least they didn't seem upset she'd been caught listening to them.

"May I have the next dance?" Lord Pennella asked, already extending his arm toward her as if she'd already said yes.

"That's a splendid idea," her mother said for her. "And while you do that, I'll find her father and talk to him."

Regina's stomach tensed as her mother hurried across the room.

"Miss Giles?"

She turned her gaze back to him and saw he was watching her expectantly. After she closed her fan, she accepted his arm and let him lead her to the floor. The music started in short time, and she scanned the room, wondering if Toby had returned yet. Whatever could be keeping him?

"I take it you heard me talking to your mother about marriage," Lord Pennella spoke up.

She swallowed, uncertain of how to answer him.

"There's no need to be embarrassed, Miss Giles. I fully intend to tell your father my intentions. I'd consider myself a fortunate gentleman to have you as my countess."

"Oh." She couldn't think of a single positive thing to say to that. He was being surprisingly forthcoming in his speech.

"There's no need to be hesitant with me. If we are to be married, we can speak freely to one another."

She scanned the room again. Still no sign of Toby. Taking a deep breath, she said, "There are other ladies who would suit you much better." There. That was a good start. Maybe if she could dissuade him, he'd change his mind.

"If there are, I'm not aware of them," he replied with that charming smile of his.

"There are many. Prettier ones. More likeable ones. Ones who would provide you with a healthy heir."

He chuckled. "If I didn't know better, I'd assume you had your mind set on someone else."

"Oh." Was she that obvious? Did he know about Toby? He had been talking to her mother for a while before she walked up behind them. Maybe her mother told him everything.

"Some gentlemen pretend to be interested in young ladies, but that's because a lot of them don't have any money and are hoping to marry for financial gain. I'm not one of them, of course. I have more than enough. My feelings for you are genuine. But I do worry that you might have mistaken Lord Davenport's attention for sincere fondness. He doesn't have any money, and it's no secret your family is one of the wealthier ones."

It took a moment for his meaning to dawn on her, and when it did, she only grew to detest him that much more. Did he really think it was appropriate to badmouth another gentleman? Even if Toby didn't have any money to his name, she still wanted to be with him. If it was true and Toby didn't tell her, it was probably because he was ashamed.

But her father had more than enough to make up for whatever Toby lacked. The important thing was that he loved her. Money could buy many things but love and a happy marriage weren't two of them.

"I know it's an unpleasant shock," Lord Pennella finally said as the music came to an end. "And I'm sorry I had to be the one to tell you, but I wanted to make sure you weren't taken in by someone who doesn't really care about you."

Refusing to meet his gaze, she curtsied then turned away. Once again, she searched for Toby but didn't find him anywhere. Well, maybe it was just as well she had to talk to him in one of the other rooms. If they could have a private conversation, they could get this straightened out, and she could tell him to let her father know his intentions before her father got attached to Lord Pennella. With a glance around to make sure no one was watching her, she skirted around the room and hurried down the hallway.

Chapter Ten

Toby poured another drink in Orlando's glass then put the decanter back on the desk. "Are you sure you want another one?"

"Give it to me," Orlando slurred.

Toby crossed the den and handed the glass to his friend. "You didn't even know Miss Boyle that well," Toby said as he sat in the chair next to his friend. "How can you be that miserable?"

"I didn't have to know everything about her to know she's perfect for me." Orlando stared at his drink but didn't take a sip. His shoulders slouched forward, and he shook his head.

"Tell her how you feel and run off with her. Couples do it from time to time."

"Don't you think I would if I could?" Orlando moaned and ran his fingers through his hair. "She's already married."

"She is?"

He nodded. "A quiet affair." His jaw clenched. "Her father didn't even tell me he had contracted her marriage last week. If I'd known, I would have done something to stop the travesty."

"But how many times did you actually talk to her?"

"We shared four dances, not all on the same day, and we talked one time in the market. But it's not the length of time you talk to someone. You can know right away whether there's something there or not."

"I hate to remind you of this, but she was dancing and flirting with every gentleman who came near her. How do you know you meant something to her?"

"A feeling. I just know." Orlando glanced at the drink and stood up. He set it on the desk. "If you truly care about Miss Giles, then don't waste any more time. Don't wait for this bet to get settled. Just marry her."

"You don't think it's too soon?" Toby would love to do nothing more than propose to her tonight, but he worried that it wasn't the right time.

"If I could go back in time, I would have proposed to Miss Boyle the night I met her."

Toby bit his tongue on a reply. Now, the same night would have been too soon. There was no denying that. But he had visited with Miss Giles twice now. She seemed to be willing to be with him. If he guessed right, she returned his feelings.

"If you really care about her, propose now before something messes things up."

"He's right," a familiar voice called out.

Toby turned and saw Toplyn enter the room. He crossed the distance between them and lowered his voice. "I just heard from Edon that Miss Giles' mother has her heart set on her marrying Pennella."

"She what?" Toby asked, feeling betrayed. Granted, he didn't really know her mother all that well, but he thought they got along well enough. What was it about Pennella that she enjoyed so much?

"Edon overheard her mother tell Pennella to introduce her father to a business acquaintance. And you know how well fathers like those kinds of connections."

Orlando came over to them. "Her father will probably want him for a son-in-law if he thinks he can financially benefit from it." He glanced at Toby. Though Orlando had been careful enough not to reveal how poor Toby was, he knew full well that Toby didn't have the same connections Pennella did. "You need to make your move. Tonight."

Toby pushed down the uneasy feeling in his gut. "Where is Miss Giles?" he asked Toplyn.

"Dancing with Pennella. They're almost done."

"Well, I'm allowed one more dance with her." Maybe he'd blurt it out and see what happened. "You think I should ask her father if I can propose first?"

"No," Orlando replied. "If the mother is all for it, her father will likely choose Pennella. What you need to do is create a scandal."

"But then he loses his estate to Pennella by default," Toplyn argued.

"Better to lose his estate than to lose Miss Giles," Orlando replied.

Toby had so little to his name, the argument was pointless. "I need to talk to Miss Giles."

"Good," Toplyn said, a relieved smile on his face. "Be quick. If you can get her to agree to marry you, you officially win the bet, regardless of what her parents say."

"I'm really going to marry her," Toby replied. "This isn't about the bet anymore. I honestly care for her."

Toplyn shrugged. "Whatever the reason, I don't care as long as you win."

After Toplyn left, Orlando went back to the desk and downed the brandy in his glass. "Love is such a fleeting thing. When you find it, you need to hold on and never let go. Forget what the others are saying. Forget the wager. Just do what is in your heart. If you need to create a scandal to secure her hand, then do it. The gentlemen at White's will just have to deal with it."

Toby took a deep breath. "I'll ask her first. I want to do right by her." Even if this whole thing started as a wager, he wanted to give her an honorable wedding.

To his surprise, Orlando came up to him and hugged him. "Good luck."

"Now I know you had too much to drink." He couldn't recall Orlando ever hugging him. "Go on home and sleep it off."

Orlando hiccupped and patted him on the shoulder. "Good idea. Let me know what happens tomorrow." He wobbled a bit as he left the room, but he managed to make it through the doorway without running into anything.

Thank goodness Orlando's coachman was waiting for him to take him home. Toby couldn't recall a time when his friend had gotten drunk. This was so unlike him. Despite the brief time he'd shared with Miss Boyle, he sure did take her marriage to another gentleman hard. Toby shouldn't be too rough with his friend, though. If Miss Giles ended up with someone else, he'd probably feel like drowning his sorrows in liquor, too.

A sound from the doorway caught his attention, and he thought Orlando had returned, but Miss Giles slipped into the room and checked the hallway before shutting the door behind her.

"What are you doing?" he whispered, glad Toplyn and Orlando left before she showed up. Unless...she had been waiting outside and heard them talking. "Did you just get here?"

"Yes. I didn't pass anyone in the hall. No one saw me."

He relaxed. "If we're caught together, it'll mean a scandal."

"I know, but I had to chance it."

She walked over to him, the candlelight bringing out the highlights in her golden hair and making her skin look especially lovely. If he hadn't had a drink to share in his friend's sorrows, he might not feel so aroused at the sight of her. But there was something about being alone with her that gave him thoughts he shouldn't have until they exchanged their vows.

When she stood in front of him, she turned those lovely green eyes to him. "You told me to call you Toby."

Since she seemed to be waiting for a response, he nodded. "I did."

"Then am I to assume a proposal is imminent?"

He blinked, not sure he'd heard her right. Was she really asking him if he planned to marry her? He studied her expression and saw she was serious.

Well, he had planned to ask her, and this was as good a time as any. It seemed unfair to rush her through a courtship. She deserved to be lavished with his time and tokens of his affection, even if those tokens weren't going to be anything extravagant.

"You'd be right to assume that," he softly admitted.

She smiled then wrapped her arms around his neck and kissed him. Actually kissed him! Unable to believe his good fortune, he didn't respond to her right away, and she pulled away from him.

"Did I do something wrong?" she asked.

"No, I just didn't expect it, that's all."

Then, before she could back away from him, he lowered his head and kissed her in return. Tightening her arms around his neck, she deepened the kiss, making no mistake that she wanted to marry him.

Bringing her into his arms, he kissed her again, realizing even as he did so that he was risking them getting caught. At the moment, nothing else mattered but the fact that she was with him. His tongue brushed her lower lip, and she opened her mouth to receive him. He let out a low, grateful groan and interlaced his tongue with hers.

She wiggled closer to him, her breasts pressing more intimately against him, an action which only excited him further. There was no way she could know the effect she was having on him. And the male part of him was insisting he throw caution right out the window and explore more of her.

His tongue sparring with hers, he brought his hands to her waist then up until they were right below her breasts. Since she didn't make a move to push him away, he ventured a little higher, aroused even more when she let out a slight gasp of pleasure. His thumbs caressed the fabric of her gown.

He took note of the soft round flesh that yielded to his touch. The ridges of her nipples hardened for him, inviting him to do more. And he was more than happy to oblige her. He cupped her breasts in his hands, lightly squeezing them, trying to memorize how they felt, wishing she didn't have her clothes on so he could lower his head and kiss her, maybe even run his tongue along her nipples and see if she'd enjoy it.

She moaned into his mouth and ran her hands down his back then cupped his behind in her hands. He figured she'd be passionate, but he had no idea she'd be so wonderfully intense. She'd be a most delightful companion in bed. His fingers traced the neckline of her gown and dipped when he came upon her cleavage. She was so soft and wonderfully feminine.

He had the sudden urge to pull the gown up to her waist, loosen the buttons on his trousers and make her his. Without a doubt, her flesh would be a most welcoming place for him to enter. And judging by the strength of his erection, it wouldn't take long for the deed to be done.

But he wouldn't take full liberties. He couldn't. She was a lady and deserved to be treated as such. Reluctant to stop, he pulled away from her, his blood racing through his body. She opened her eyes and looked at him. Her cheeks were flushed, her lips swollen from their kisses, her breathing fast. He couldn't resist the urge to look at her breasts which strained against her neckline.

Clearing his throat, he returned his gaze to hers. He clasped her hands in his and said the first thing that came to mind. "Will you marry me?"

"Yes, Toby. I'll marry you." She squeezed his hands, her smile growing wider. "And you should call me Regina."

"Regina. That's a wonderful name." Unable to stop the grin that crossed his face, he brought her back into his arms and kissed her. "I'm the happiest gentleman in all of London."

"Will you talk to my father tomorrow about marrying me?"

"Yes." He paused. "Do you think he'll let me marry you?"

"As long as you let him know your intentions tomorrow, he will."

"Then I'll do that." He gave her another kiss then released her. "We should get out of here before someone catches us. I don't want to ruin your reputation. You go first and I'll wait a few minutes and leave. Then we can have our second dance."

"All right."

She gave him a quick kiss before she hurried out. He couldn't believe his good fortune. Nothing could spoil this for him. Not Pennella. Not the gentlemen at White's who lost the bet and would be upset. Not anyone. Everything was perfect.

THE NEXT MORNING, TOBY'S world came crashing down around him. As soon as he got to White's, the gentlemen were either snickering, shaking their heads in sympathy, or bemoaning the fact that the bet was now annulled.

"What's going on?" he asked the Duke of Ashbourne who was reading something in the *Tittletattle*.

The duke's gaze met his, and he patted his shoulder. "I'm sorry, Davenport."

Before Toby could ask him what he was talking about, he handed him his copy of the scandal sheet.

"If it's any consolation, at least you don't have to risk your entire estate to someone like Pennella," he added then headed for another room.

In dread, Toby's attention went to the front page of the *Tittletattle*. This couldn't be good. There was no way it could be good. He braced himself and read the first item on the sheet.

Lord Davenport has made a bet with Lord Pennella. The wager? The hand of Miss Giles. Whoever marries her gains the loser's estate.

His gaze went lower. Someone named Gerard Addison had reported it.

For a moment, Toby couldn't breathe. This was the worst thing that could possibly happen. Last evening had gone so well. He had proposed to Regina, and she had said yes. This afternoon, he was supposed to go over to her townhouse and make his intentions known to her father. Then he was supposed to forget the wager, marry her, and live happily ever after. But as he reread the lines on the paper, he realized nothing was going to play out like he hoped because once Regina saw this...

He felt as if he'd been punched in the gut. As soon as Regina saw this, she might not want to marry him. And who could blame her? She'd never believe he was sincere when he told her he wanted to be with her. Now, she was going to assume he only said it to win the bet. He'd think the same thing in her position.

"What's the meaning of this?" Pennella yelled as he ran into the room, holding a copy of the *Tittletattle* in his hands. He waved it in the air and glared at everyone who dared to make eye contact with him. "Who told the *Ttitletattle* about the wager?"

Not surprising, everyone kept silent.

"Someone in this gentlemen's club did it," Pennella snapped, rolling the paper up and slamming it on the nearby table.

"There's no Gerard Addison at White's," Roderick argued.

"You take me for a fool? I know very well that Gerard isn't the gentleman's real name. No one would dare give their real name if they wrote for this garbage." He released the *Tittletattle* and looked around the room where about twenty gentlemen were all reading copies of the paper. Finally, his gaze settled on Toby. "You? Did you do this because I made a connection with Miss Giles' father? You did this because you knew you were going to lose?"

"Of course, I didn't do it," Toby replied, not hiding his anger. Did Pennella really think this made him happy?

"Then who did?"

"I don't know!"

The room remained silent as Pennella studied everyone's faces. "When I find out who's behind this, he's going to wish he was never born."

No one responded as Pennella stormed out of White's and slammed the door. It'd been tense. But it was nowhere as bad as Toby knew it was going to be when he saw Regina...when he pleaded with her to marry him despite the wager.

He could avoid her and try to forget he ever met her, but he loved her. There would never be anyone but her. He owed it to both of them to try—to beg her to give him another chance. Steeling his resolve, he hurried out of White's.

Chapter Eleven

Regina was sorting through her outfits, trying to decide which one would be best for a horseback ride with Toby. In a couple hours, he'd come by, and this time, there would be talk about the banns and a wedding date.

"Miss Giles."

Glancing at the partly open door, she smiled at her lady's maid. "I know it's silly, but I can't wait to see Lord Davenport."

She couldn't be sure, but it seemed that the older woman slightly winced.

"Is something wrong?" Regina asked.

"Your parents wish to see you in the drawing room."

Surprised by her solemn tone, she closed the armoire and rushed down the stairs. Did something bad happen? Was someone in their family ill? By the time she reached the drawing room, her parents were reading something. Their faces were pale, and they stood as still as statues.

"What is it? What's happened?" Regina asked as she hurried over to them.

With a heavy sigh, her father shook his head and plopped down in one of the chairs.

Her mother closed the distance between them and handed her the *Tittletattle*. "It's right at the top."

She almost asked her what was at the top but saw 'Lord Davenport' and kept reading. *Lord Davenport has made a bet with Lord Pennella.*

The wager? The hand of Miss Giles. Whoever marries her gains the loser's estate.

After her mother closed the door, she returned to Regina. "Did you know about the wager?"

She looked up from the *Tittletattle* but couldn't speak. Her legs shaky, she went over to the settee and collapsed on it. After a moment, she read the tidbit of gossip again, hoping it would be different this time. But it was the same thing she'd read before.

"Do you know Gerard Addison?" her mother pressed, leaning over her.

"No," Regina forced out. "I don't know Gerard Addison."

"Did you know about the wager?"

Tears formed in Regina's eyes. "No. How could you think I'd know about something this...this..." Good heavens, but she couldn't even think of the right word to describe it.

"Well, you were involved in it."

"Not directly." She blinked and a couple tears fell down her cheeks. "I didn't know what they were doing. I thought they were both..."

Her face grew warm from a mixture of humiliation and anger. How foolish. After not receiving much interest until recently, why didn't she suspect something was amiss when two gentlemen suddenly sought her attention—and at the same time. It was so obvious when she looked back on it. She wiped away more tears.

"She couldn't have known," her father said, his voice soothing. "If she had, she never would have let them pay her a visit."

Her mother relaxed but only slightly. "Of course, you're right." She settled next to Regina and cupped her elbow in her hand. "This is horrible. Just horrible."

With a shaky breath, Regina nodded. Her chances of finding a good titled gentleman were gone. Even if she hadn't enjoyed the way her mother fussed over her, she couldn't blame her mother for being devastated. But it was much worse than the shock of learning about the wager. Everything Toby had said and done was based on lies. It was all so he could win a bet. It had nothing to do with his feelings for her.

"What should we do?" her mother asked her father.

"Hold Lord Davenport to a proposal. Regina said he wished to speak to me about marriage. We'll make him go through with it."

Regina's head snapped in his direction. "No! I can't marry him."

"Why not? He's a titled gentleman," he began.

"None of his feelings were sincere."

"I wouldn't be so sure about that. He had a certain way of looking at you that spoke volumes of how he felt."

"When he looked at me, he saw the wealth you have." Her gaze went to her mother. "You know how titled gentlemen are when they need money. They don't care who they marry if it'll save their troubled estate."

A knock at the door interrupted them.

Her mother groaned. "Why does someone always have to come over when there's something important going on?" Shaking her head, she went to the door.

Regina glanced at her father whose sympathetic expression did little to ease her heartache.

Her mother opened the door and spoke in low tones to the butler. Her gaze went to Regina, and Regina stiffened. What else could possibly go wrong? Hadn't she been through enough already?

"No," she heard her mother tell the butler. "Absolutely not."

Before Regina could ask what her mother was saying no to, the butler stepped aside and Toby came into view. The *Tittletattle* crumpled in her grip.

"Please, let me talk to her," Toby pressed. "I can explain everything."

"We know all about the wager," her mother replied. "There's nothing to explain."

"Let him come in," her father spoke up, rising to his feet. Startled, Regina shook her head in protest, but he put up his hand to stop her before she could say anything. "If he intends to make things right, we'll let him," he said in a voice low enough so the others wouldn't overhear. "Give him a chance."

Give him a chance? Was her father daft? Like she wanted to talk to Toby ever again, let alone marry him!

"Regina," her father whispered, "I know this is not an ideal situation, but think this through before you tell him no. This is all over the Ton. If you don't secure a husband now, it's doubtful you will after this."

"But he only wants your money."

"Money might have been the primary motive, but his feelings for you are true. I have no doubt of that."

Her poor father was seeing things that weren't there. It'd all been a show. Everything Toby had done and said... How could she have fallen for it? Because she wanted—more than anything—to believe that a love match was possible, even in a society as polluted with greed and selfishness as this one.

Her father patted her on the shoulder. "The choice is yours, of course. But if nothing else, you'd be a countess and would have children."

He turned to Toby and asked him to have a seat beside her on the settee. Then he took her mother by the elbow and escorted her out of the drawing room.

After her father shut the door, she bolted to her feet and headed for the window. What had her father been thinking by inviting Toby to be so close to her?

"Will you please sit?" Toby asked.

Crossing her arms, Regina said, "I'll remain standing, thank you."

She needed to keep as much distance between them as possible. It was the only way to keep her thoughts clear. Because even now—even after finding out about the horrible wager—the sight of him made her weak in the knees. And that wasn't good. It made her vulnerable, something she didn't like one single bit.

When Toby approached her, she had the urge to bolt for the door but managed to stay still. Showing him any weakness wouldn't be good.

"Whatever you have to say, you can say from where you are," she said before he could take another step toward her.

"Regina-"

"It's Miss Giles to you."

He paused for a moment then nodded. "I deserve that. I know what I did was wrong, and you have every right to be upset."

"Why did you do it?" she blurted out, watching him as he shifted uncomfortably a mere few feet from her.

"Well," he slowly began, "Pennella barged into White's and claimed he could get any lady he wanted. It's not the first time he made the boast, but it was the first time I had enough of it. I decided to stand up to him, and before I knew what was happening, I was stuck in the wager. I made the stipulation that I would pick the lady-"

"Lucky me," she muttered.

He sighed. "I didn't intend to actually marry you."

"What?" She didn't think it was possible to feel worse, but she did.

"I didn't mean it like that."

"It's hard to take that in a good way." Especially after how close they'd gotten.

"My intention was to protect you from Pennella. The only way I could do that was to make you choose me, but," he quickly added when she opened her mouth to protest, "I was going to let you go. I wasn't going to hold you to a marriage. That wouldn't have been fair to you. But then I got to know you and fell in love with you. I know it's hard to believe, but when I asked you to marry me, I did mean it."

"It is hard to believe."

"I can't blame you for feeling that way, but it's true. And I still want to marry you. Will you please be my wife?"

"No."

She couldn't believe it, but he actually looked surprised by her answer. "No?" he asked.

"No." When he didn't reply, she added, "Did you expect me to say yes after you made a fool of me?"

Shoulders slumped, he shook his head. "No, I didn't expect you to say yes."

"Then why did you act so surprised?"

"I had hoped... Never mind. This is a mess, and it's one of my doing. I wasn't supposed to fall in love with you, but I did."

She turned away from him and looked out the window. She didn't want to hear it. For all she knew, this could be another one of his lies. There was nothing—absolutely nothing—she could believe anymore. He'd made a complete fool of her. And worse, everyone knew her shame. She swallowed and quickly wiped away the tear that slid down her cheek. The last thing she needed was to appear weak. She couldn't do anything about what Toby or Pennella did, but she could control how she reacted to it. And there was no way she was going to let anyone know how much this hurt her.

"Miss Giles," Toby softly began as he approached her, "I'm sorry. I know nothing can undo the damage I've done." He waited for a long moment before he continued. "I do love you. Despite how everything looks, it's true. And you did agree to marry me last night. I was to ask your father for your hand today."

"That was before I found out the truth," she snapped, glaring at him. Then, before another tear would trickle down her cheek, she turned her attention back to the people outside. It was much easier to avoid further humiliation if she counted them. After a few seconds passed, she was able to take a deep breath to steady her resolve. "We have nothing more to say to each other. You may go."

She expected him to leave. She'd refused him, made it clear that there was no way she'd marry him. But he didn't leave. He stayed right where he was. She could feel the heat of his gaze as he watched her.

And honestly, she didn't know if she was glad he chose to stay or not. It was too hard to tell what she should be feeling when her emotions were swirling around her in such a frantic mess.

"I understand you don't want to marry me because of what I've done," he said, his hesitant tone indicating that he was choosing his words carefully. "But I think a marriage is the best course."

She snorted, something that was horribly unladylike. Her mother would have fainted on the spot had she heard it.

"Please hear me out before you dismiss the idea."

She sighed but didn't argue. Instead, she continued counting the people as they walked along the side of the street.

After a tense moment, he spoke up. "I have a title. If we marry, then you could satisfy your mother and your son will inherit my title."

"If I have a son." She quickly shut her mouth. It wasn't in her best interest to say anything at the moment.

"Yes, that's true. There's always the possibility we'll only have girls."

"And there's also the possibility you'll never be in my bed," she added then admonished herself. The more she talked, the greater the potential was for her to say something she could never take back.

"Well, I suppose that's also true. But then it won't matter if you won't have a son anyway. My title would go to my cousin. But you will still be a countess."

When she didn't reply, he took another step toward her. As much as she wanted to back away from him, she refused to budge another inch. It was bad enough she was trapped between two undesirable options.

Her chances of securing a marriage to an honorable gentleman were now nil. And that left her with her mother who would undoubtedly spend the rest of her living years lamenting this incident. But if she married him, her mother would eventually forget all about this black mark on her life.

She debated living out the remainder of her years as a spinster. No doubt, her mother would grow wearisome. Her father would pity her. Unless she wanted to have this moment hanging over her head forever, she had to marry him. There was no other way out. Blinking back her tears before he could see them, she steeled her resolve.

"Fine," she finally said, her voice steady despite her fear that she'd regret this decision in the years to come. "I'll marry you." Before he could reply, she turned a sharp gaze in his direction. "But this isn't a love match. It's one borne out of necessity."

Though he winced, he nodded. "That's fair."

"Then the bargain is struck. I marry you so I can be a countess, and you marry me so you can get the money." His jaw dropped, so she added, "Yes, I know your estate's in trouble. But I'd been willing to marry you anyway. Now, I'm just marrying you because it's better than spending the rest of my life with an unhappy mother."

Forcing aside her moment's regret that things had to be this way, she strode to the door. How she managed to walk at all surprised her. She guessed with everything happening so fast, she was in a state of shock. Such a thing made sense, of course...all things considered.

Opening the door, she paused when she saw her parents standing in front of her, both looking as if they'd been caught doing something they weren't supposed to. "Were you eavesdropping on me?" she asked.

Her mother let out an uneasy chuckle. "No. We were waiting here in case you called for assistance. You have been through a terrible ordeal, and we're your parents. Your wellbeing is important to us."

She eyed them both, suspecting they had been listening but unable to prove it. Well, what did it matter? Her reputation was already ruined. It wasn't like they were going to make things worse. "All right," she relented. "You might as well be the first to know that Lord Davenport has asked for my hand in marriage and I've accepted."

"That is a prudent decision," her father replied in relief.

"I don't know," her mother whispered, her gaze flickering to the drawing room.

Regina glanced over her shoulder where Toby stood by the window, watching them but not interfering with their conversation. Turning her attention back to her mother, she lowered her voice. "What choice do I have, Mother? My reputation is in ruins. No one else will propose unless he's a reprobate."

"Of all the options available to her, this is the smartest one," her father told her mother.

Her mother sighed. "I suppose so."

"Well," her father said with a smile as he turned to Toby, "it's only appropriate that I welcome you to the family."

Toby glanced from Regina to her father then slowly walked over to them. "Thank you, sir."

Her father patted him on the back and chuckled. "There's no need to stand on formality now that we'll be family. You can think of me as a friend."

"Oh, well, that's very nice of you."

Regina averted her gaze and chose to look at her mother who decided not to extend a welcome. She couldn't blame her mother. This was hardly the happy occasion she imagined it would be a mere hour ago when she was in her bedchamber making plans for a wedding and her new life with Toby. Now that all seemed to be a distant memory.

"Let's discuss the details of the wedding while Regina and her mother look for a suitable dress," her father said.

Regina glanced at her father. Did he really think it was appropriate to go through the ceremony as if nothing horrible had happened?

To her surprise, her mother offered a curt nod. "Yes, that would be best."

Before Regina could utter one word of protest, her mother took her by the arm and led her out of the drawing room, choosing to shut the door so the gentlemen could have their privacy. Then her mother summoned the butler and instructed him to get the coachman.

"You can't be serious, Mother," Regina whispered while she followed her mother up the stairs. "You want to go shopping for a wedding dress? Under these circumstances?"

Her mother didn't answer her until they reached the top of the staircase. "No, I don't want to shop for one, but what choice do we have? Even in the midst of tragedy, a lady is expected to look her best. You might have a tattered reputation, but you'll still be one of the most beautiful brides London has ever seen. Now, get your gloves and hat then meet me at the carriage."

With nothing else to do, she headed for her bedchamber. When she opened the door, she caught sight of the armoire where she'd been sorting through her riding clothes, trying to decide which one to wear for horseback riding. A tear slid down her cheek, and she quickly wiped it away. It was supposed to be a good afternoon, the kind she'd later tell her children about when they asked if a love match was possible when so few people seemed to believe in it.

And now, what was she supposed to tell them? That marriages were done solely out of convenience? That she offered money and Toby offered a title? That it was nothing more than a cold transaction, one in which she was forced into because of a bet?

Wiping away another tear, she gathered her gloves and hat. The day hadn't gone as planned. And there was nothing she could do about it. All she could do was make the future as bearable as possible. She wasn't sure what that meant yet, but she was determined that she would never be played for a fool again. No matter what, she wouldn't let Toby close enough to hurt her a second time.

Chapter Twelve

From the window in the drawing room, Toby watched Regina and her mother walk down the steps of the townhouse and go to the carriage waiting out front. He swallowed, wondering if he'd just doomed both him and Regina to a life of misery. He didn't deserve her. She'd been skeptical of gentlemen before, but she'd opened her heart to him, showing him that there was a part of her that could trust someone who claimed to love her. And now in light of the wager, she'd closed herself back up.

This was a mess of his own doing. If only he'd kept his mouth shut when Pennella was bragging about his prowess with the ladies, she would've been spared the grief he was now putting her through. His jaw clenched as he recalled how pale her face had been when he asked her to marry him today. It was so different from her response yesterday. Now, it seemed like a business transaction instead of a love match. Who knew if she'd ever allow him into her heart again?

"Don't let my daughter trouble you."

Turning his gaze to Mr. Giles, he said, "She has every right to detest me."

Her father shrugged. "She'll get over it."

"I don't see how."

"You love her. I could tell that from the first time I met you. You've made her happy. I can't recall a time she smiled or laughed before she met you. Whatever circumstances brought you two together are of little consequence. The important thing is, you two will be happy."

"I doubt it," he mumbled.

"Ladies are fickle creatures. One day, they're upset. The next, they can't remember why. It's how they are. Their moods swing from one extreme to the other, and most of the time, a gentleman can't figure out why." He chuckled and came up beside him. "I remember one day when Regina was a little girl. She wanted so much to go to the circus. She was excited the whole way there. But when we were there, she grew bored and wanted to leave. Ever since, she hasn't had the slightest desire to go back. Why? Who can say? She said she just realized it wasn't as entertaining as she'd heard. That's ridiculous, of course. I'm amused every time I go there."

It suddenly dawned on Toby what the older gentleman was doing. He was trying to ease his doubts about proposing to Regina. With a smile, he said, "She has every right to be upset with me."

"Oh, I'm not saying she doesn't. A lady doesn't like to be betted on. But you know, there are worse things that could happen to her. She could have drunk some poison or got run over by a horse. The possibilities of what could happen are endless."

Toby wasn't sure what drinking poison or being run over by a horse had to do with this mess, but her father was showing him kindness—a kindness he didn't deserve—so he was willing to listen to anything he wanted to say.

"You don't have any sisters, do you?" her father asked.

"No. I'm an only child."

"A shame. The same thing is true with Regina. I wanted to have more children, but her mother came ill shortly after she was born and wasn't able to conceive after that. I hope you two will have a house full of children. It's good for children to grow up with brothers or sisters. They have someone they can play with." He paused then offered a shrug. "But anyway, what I wanted to say is that if you'd had a sister, you would be accustomed to the way ladies change their minds. You'd be prepared for it. Since you've had no such experience, this thing with my daughter looks worse than it is."

"I hope you're right."

"Of course, I'm right. I've been with her mother for twenty-three years, and if there's ever a lady who ends up seeing the best in things after swearing up and down she doesn't like it, it's her. She might be headstrong, but she's reasonable when given enough time to come around. Regina will be the same way. Now," he gestured to the chair, "sit down and tell me about yourself. Who are your parents? Where did you go to school? What are your plans for the future? What will you name your children? Tell me anything that's on your mind."

Toby followed him to the chairs and answered all the questions her father had.

"YOU WANT TO GO FOR a walk?" Regina's mother asked a couple days later. "Are you sure that's wise?"

Regina slipped on her gloves as she stood by the front door. "I can't stay inside forever." She'd spent the past couple days inside, hiding from the rest of the world, aware that all of London was laughing over the wager Toby and Lord Pennella made at her expense. But she was tired of hiding. She needed to get out and be a part of the world again, even if it was going to be difficult. "The sooner I go back out there, the easier it'll be," she added, more for herself than for her mother's benefit.

"Then I'll come with you."

"No." When she caught the hurt look in her mother's eyes, she smiled to soften the blow. "I need to do this alone."

Her mother returned her smile then rubbed her arm. "All right."

Regina indicated to the footman that she was ready, and he opened the door. She slipped outside, squinting at the bright sunlight. After she adjusted her bonnet, she walked down the steps and headed down the sidewalk. She had no particular destination in mind. She just needed to get out of the townhouse and remind herself that life went on even in the middle of unpleasant circumstances.

But as she proceeded through the streets, she became aware that people were staring at her and whispering to each other. She already knew what they were whispering about. They were whispering about her, and more specifically, the wager between Toby and Lord Pennella. She turned her gaze from the people, pretending that nothing they said bothered her. Once she let them know they could upset her, it would only be worse. But if she acted like nothing was wrong, they would drop the matter sooner. Or at least that's what she hoped.

She made it to a nice pathway in the park and was glad for the reprieve. The trees provided a good place to hide. Finding a private bench without anyone nearby, she settled on it and closed her eyes. A cool breeze blew around her, and she felt herself relax. She didn't realize she'd been so tense, but it didn't surprise her. What lady would want to be snared into a scandal of this sort?

She opened her eyes and took in the flowers and trees. One nice thing about trees and flowers was that they didn't care what people thought. They simply grew and blossomed every spring regardless of the circumstances surrounding them. After several minutes, her mind finally settled on more pleasant things, and she found reasons to be grateful. She had her health. She had parents who loved her. Despite her mother's faults, the lady did want the best for her. And truth be told, she had been deeply moved by her mother's concern for her that morning. Sometimes it was easy to lose sight of how much her mother cared in the midst of her busy life, though her mother's ploy to get Lord Pennella into her father's good graces still bothered her.

If Toby had engaged her in gossip, she would have been hoping Regina would marry him instead. But he hadn't engaged in such gossip, nor did he try to charm her with false flattery. Of the two, Toby was still the better choice.

As much as she tried to deny it, the memory of Toby's kiss still made her toes tingle. Had it been anyone else, she wouldn't have risked getting caught alone with a gentleman in such a compromising situation.

But she had been willing to risk a scandal if it meant she could marry him. With a roll of her eyes, she chuckled at the irony. She'd gotten her scandal all right, though it wasn't in the way she hoped.

She took a deep breath and released it. She really thought he was different. But who knew what he was really like? For all she knew, he enjoyed gossip as much as Lord Pennella.

She rubbed her forehead. If she wasn't careful, she was going to get a headache. She'd gotten plenty of those in the past couple days, and God knew she was tired of crying. It wasn't going to change anything.

Maybe now that the lies had been exposed, Toby would start being who he truly was. She could only pray that he wasn't the bad sort, but what kind of gentleman wagered a lady's fate for the sake of money? Could such a gentleman be trusted?

Gritting her teeth, she wiped her tears away. How she hated crying. It was a weakness, and she had often prided herself on being strong. She didn't want to be a pitiful lady who fell at a gentleman's feet and did whatever he wanted. She wanted to be her husband's equal. She wanted to be respected, for her wishes to be important to him, to be loved. And now it felt as if she would have none of it.

Swallowing back more tears, she decided she might as well go back home. Going outside had been a mistake. Who wanted to watch a lady cry on a bench while she bemoaned her fate? No one. And quite frankly, she didn't want to watch them shoot her their looks of pity either.

Just as she got ready to stand up, someone called out a greeting to her. She bristled for a moment then realized it wasn't a male's voice. Good. She didn't want to see Toby right now, not when she felt like she'd whack him on the head for what he did.

Her gaze went to the left, and she saw Lady Seyton with Miss Boyle. Forcing a smile, she motioned to the spot next to her. "Good afternoon."

They sat next to her, and Lady Seyton leaned toward her. "How are you doing?"

"As well as can be expected," Regina replied. "At least I secured a marriage like my parents wanted."

Shooting her a sympathetic smile, Lady Seyton touched her arm. Regina blinked, surprised at the kind gesture. She didn't take Lady Seyton for a compassionate lady, but apparently, there was more to her than met the eye. "A scandal isn't the way I was hoping to get you engaged."

"I know." Regina shrugged and stared at her hands. "I should have known something was wrong when I had two gentlemen pursuing me."

"Nonsense. You had every right to believe they were sincere. You followed my instructions, and you are beautiful with a wealthy father. All those things attract titled gentlemen. You couldn't help the wager that was going on at White's." She shook her head. "Gentlemen just have too much time on their hands if they're going to do such revolting things."

"It is insulting," Miss Boyle agreed. "I'm very sorry."

Regina smiled. "Thank you, Miss Boyle. And you're right. It is insulting. We're ladies, not cards in a gambling hell."

"Good analogy," Lady Seyton replied. "Please call me Helena. As for Miss Boyle, she has married Lord Hawkins."

"Oh, I didn't realize." Regina glanced at her. "Forgive me, Lady Hawkins."

"Call me Chloe," she said.

"I don't know either of you very well," Regina hesitantly responded. "Are you sure being so intimate is a good idea?"

"I get tired of being called Lady Seyton all the time," Helena said. "Given, it's a memorial to my departed husband. But I prefer to be called by my Christian name. Besides, I feel like I know you well enough after giving you those lessons in how to attract gentlemen."

"Yes, I suppose you're right." Though it was hard for Regina to think of her as a friend. The lady wasn't that much older than her, but she was a widow and had more experience than she did.

"She's not as intimidating as she initially appears," Chloe chimed in.

"Intimidating?" Helena glanced at Regina. "You don't think I'm intimidating, do you?"

"Do you want the truth?" Regina asked, a slight teasing tone finding its way into her voice despite her circumstances.

Helena sighed. "I don't see what's so intimidating about me. I do what I can to help others."

"But you know so much, and we don't," Chloe said.

Regina relaxed. So she wasn't the only one who had been overwhelmed by how much Helena understood gentlemen. "You do have a lot more knowledge than we do."

"That's only because I was married," Helena replied. "It has nothing to do with being born with some grand insight. I just had a husband who didn't mind telling me what gentlemen liked and didn't like. I take that information and pass it on to others."

"Did you have a love match then?" Chloe wondered, her wide eyes directed at Helena.

"Well, not really. We were very comfortable with each other. We'd grown up together, and it made sense to marry when we were of age." She shrugged. "Our parents were satisfied with the match. They were good friends. Their hope was that we'd have children, notably a boy, to pass on his title, but it wasn't meant to be."

"Why not?" Regina softly asked. "What happened to him?"

"He died in a duel," Helena said, her voice lower than before.

"A duel? Isn't that illegal?" Regina replied.

"That doesn't mean some gentlemen don't still practice it. The gentleman in question suggested I had been behaving inappropriately, and my husband defended me. One thing led to another, and he felt honor bound to protect my good name."

"Did you behave inappropriately?" Chloe whispered.

"Not in the way I'd been accused. The gentleman said I'd taken a lover, but what I'd been doing was giving a gentleman advice on how he might woo a lady he was interested in. This lady happened to be someone the first gentleman was also interested in. I suspect that had something to do with the allegation."

"Oh dear." Chloe sighed. "How awful."

"It's why I don't give lessons to gentlemen. I only give them to ladies. No one will take that the wrong way, nor can they use it against me."

Regina nodded, thinking that was a smart move on her part. She'd do the same thing if she was her.

"It was nice of your husband to defend you," Chloe said.

"Yes, it was," Regina agreed.

"While it was nice," Helena began, "it was unnecessary. I had nothing to be ashamed of, and he knew it. But when gentlemen get their tempers flared up, they make irrational decisions. It certainly wasn't worth dying for." She offered Regina another smile. "The wager wasn't your fault. You couldn't help what the pride of these gentlemen led them to do."

"I know," Regina replied. After a moment of silence, she glanced at Chloe. "So you're married?"

"Yes," Chloe said. "My father arranged it in a contract. I wish I had known of Helena's reputation for securing proposals before I agreed to the thing."

"Why? Aren't you happy with the gentleman your father selected?"

"I don't really know him. We married two days ago with a special license then he left for India after the wedding breakfast," Chloe replied.

"That soon? But wasn't he interested in the," Helena glanced around, "wedding night?"

"Our marriage is in name only. I had hoped for something of a love match, but my family needed the money and I ran out of time."

"If your family gets the money and you get the title, what does your husband get out of it?"

"An heir at some point."

"If the heir is so important, why didn't he try for one right away? It's not like it takes much time or effort."

Chloe's cheeks grew pink. "The lady's time of month is upon me."

"Oh." Helena chuckled. "Well, there's no getting around that one."

"He had to take care of a business venture, so it wasn't like he was disappointed."

Regina didn't know if she envied Chloe's situation or not. While it might be nice to have Toby run off for another country right after their marriage so she wouldn't have to be constantly reminded of the wager, she didn't like to think that a business venture took precedence over her.

"Regina?"

Helena's concern brought her attention back to the two ladies sitting with her. "I'm sorry. What is it?" Regina asked.

"We were wondering if you'd like to join us at my townhouse for tea," Helena replied.

She nodded. "I would. Thank you."

It'd be nice to keep talking to them. It might even help to put her impending marriage to Toby aside for a while. When she didn't think about him, she didn't feel like crying. And even if that was a small reprieve, it was one she desperately wanted. Standing up, she joined them as they proceeded to Helena's townhouse.

Chapter Thirteen

Toby stared out the window in the townhouse he rented. God knew he couldn't afford to buy one, though now that he was going to marry Regina, he could. At the moment, he felt it was enough to use the money her father had given him to hire a staff to clean up his estate. The last thing he wanted was for her to cry in despair at how much work it needed.

He'd been honest with her father, letting him know his financial position. Even if his father's reckless spending got him in this predicament, he didn't mention it. He could easily shift the blame, but he didn't feel like it. His father had made horrible wagers and lost them, and Toby couldn't say he was any better. Maybe it was selfish, but he would have made the wager all over again just for the chance to meet Regina. He wouldn't have sought her out otherwise.

Focusing on the street in front of him, he saw his friend coming up the front steps. Turning from the window, he headed for the door, only remembering that he now had a footman by the time he reached it.

The footman was opening the door just as Toby reached the entryway.

"Did you come over for a drink?" Toby asked his friend as he led him to the drawing room.

"No. I've had enough of brandy for a while. My head is still pounding from all the drink I had at Toplyn's ball."

Despite his grim mood, Toby chuckled. "I can't remember seeing you drunk."

Sitting, Orlando rested his head on the back of the chair and let out a long sigh. "Nor will you ever again. It wasn't worth it. I woke up feeling worse than I did before I took my first drink."

Toby sat across from him and crossed his arms. "I'd say things didn't work out the way either one of us hoped."

"Well, they say misery loves company." He arched an eyebrow and glanced over at him. "I didn't see you at White's. In fact, no one has seen you there since the day the wager was announced in the *Tittletattle*."

"I see no reason to subject myself to further embarrassment."

"I don't blame you. I wouldn't want to go back there either. But Pennella's there."

"What's he doing now? Trying to enact another wager?"

"Nope. He's trying to figure out who exposed the one you two had. So far, he's been threatening Roderick and Edon within an inch of their lives if he finds out they're behind it."

Toby shook his head. "He needs to let the matter go. It doesn't matter how anyone found out." What mattered was that it hurt Regina.

"That's the difference between you and Pennella. You're worried about her, and he's worried about himself."

The butler came in with a tray of tea and scones.

Toby waited until the butler left before he turned his gaze back to his friend. "She hates me."

"I'm sure she won't hate you forever."

"That's what her father says, but she won't see me. I went over there three times, but each time, she's either resting or out."

"You can't expect her to come around right away." Orlando picked up the teapot and poured tea into their cups. "I think it's normal to expect a period where she'll avoid you. In a way, it's a compliment."

"Really?"

"Sure." He handed Toby the cup then picked up his own. "It means she cares for you. If she didn't care, she wouldn't react as strongly as she is."

"I don't know. Anyone would be angry over this."

Orlando sipped some tea then picked up a scone. "Maybe you're right. Maybe she never cared about you. Maybe she only wanted you for your title."

"She did care," Toby quickly replied before realizing his friend had been baiting him. "I get your point. I suppose you're right. The wager hurt even more because she did want to marry me."

"Right. I guarantee you that she's more upset with you than Pennella, and he's the one who instigated it."

"Maybe, but I didn't have to go along with it. I should have refused to play his game."

Orlando bit into the scone and swallowed. "These are good." He inspected it as if not believing the scone could taste so good.

"The butler is no longer acting as my cook," Toby explained.

"That's a relief."

"I'm sure he's as glad as you are about it."

"Probably." Then he shot him an amused glance. "You know I'm your friend because I was willing to eat the ones he used to make."

Toby chuckled. "Yes, I know. And you drank the tea."

"I am a true martyr. I sacrifice so much for my friends."

Feeling a little better, Toby drank some tea. "Are you going to be at my wedding?"

"Of course. I wouldn't miss it for anything." He finished the scone and sat back in the chair. "At least you'll get to marry her. Sure, things are bound to be shaky at first, but in time, things will work out."

Toby could only hope his friend was right, though he still didn't see how he could make amends for what he'd done.

"It's better than not having a chance," Orlando added, his tone turning serious. "I just found out that Miss Boyle married Lord Hawkins."

"Lord Hawkins?" Toby barely recalled the name but didn't remember where he'd heard it.

"He does a lot of travel to other countries and is wealthier than most. Compared to him, I never had a chance." He drank his tea and set the cup on his knee. "I offered her father my hand to her in marriage, but he said he was considering all her suitors. Now I know why I never heard a response."

"I didn't know you asked for her hand."

"What's the point? He didn't accept it. He accepted Lord Hawkins' request instead."

"I'm sorry."

"It is what it is. He who has the most money gets the lady." When Toby raised his eyebrows, he amended, "For some of us. Others get her by chance or scandal."

"While I hate to agree with you, it fits." After a long moment of silence passed between them, Toby asked, "Want to play some chess?"

"Why not? I haven't played it for a while. It might be fun."

"At least it'll take our mind off our troubles."

Waving his friend to join him, Toby went over to the table where the chessboard waited for them.

"WILL YOU PLEASE SEE Toby?" Regina's father asked a few days later.

"I'll see him tomorrow," Regina replied as she worked on her embroidery.

It wasn't that she was particularly fond of making pretty patterns with a thread and needle, but she needed something to do with her time or she'd get restless. The closer she got to the wedding, the more nervous she became. And embroidery helped take her mind off her doubts.

Her father crossed the drawing room and settled in front of the settee where she sat. "Regina, you can't avoid him forever."

"The wedding is tomorrow. I'll see him then."

"Be reasonable. He's your betrothed. You can't treat him like this."

She shot him a pointed look. "He didn't mind treating me like a pawn for another gentleman's estate."

"Sometimes people do things in a moment of weakness, but really, it could have been worse. He could have taken your virtue and left you with child, or he could have made you his mistress. But he didn't do that. He's trying to do right by you."

"I didn't realize you considered him such a hero."

"He's not a bad gentleman, and if you give him a chance, you'll realize that. Now," he rose to his feet, "I insist you see him."

"You what?" she asked, alarmed.

"You're my daughter, and you're not married yet. I still have some authority over you, and I'm using it this last time. That poor gentleman has been here to see you every day since you agreed to marry him. The least you can do is spend a little of your time with him."

Before she could respond, he was already on his way to the door. She scanned the room, wondering if there was a suitable hiding place, but alas, there was none, and all she could do was wait as her father welcomed Toby into the townhouse. It took all her willpower to remain seated as Toby entered the room, his hands behind his back.

Even after the betrayal, he could still make her heartbeat quicken at the mere sight of him. It was unfair. If she didn't love him, it'd be much easier to do this.

"Thank you for seeing me," he said as he approached her. "I hope you don't mind, but I brought these for you."

Her gaze went to his hands as he showed her the flowers. They would have been a lovely gesture if not for the wager. "Thank you," she forced out, fighting the tears that wanted to well up to the surface. He was only doing it because he felt guilty. It had nothing to do with his feelings for her.

"I'll get a vase for those, my lord," the butler said.

Toby handed him the flowers and waited until the butler left before asking, "May I sit?"

Who was going to stop him? If she said no, her father would probably march into the room and demand she say yes. She nodded but didn't say anything. Then, in case she gave her feelings away, she turned her gaze to the pattern she was sewing.

After a moment, he sat next to her, something that made her squirm a bit. She hadn't thought that being married to him would require her to be so close to him. It was silly, of course. They would have to be close. At the very least, they would sit together in a carriage. She didn't know how she was supposed to do it. Maybe they could live in separate places. It might be the only way she was going to get through this marriage.

"Words can't begin to express how truly sorry I am," he said, his voice low so no one would overhear. "I can hardly sleep or eat. I know I hurt you, and there's nothing I can do to go back in time and change things. Believe me, I would if I could."

A long pause passed between them until she realized he was waiting for her reply. She didn't know what he wanted her to say. Did he want her to lie and say it didn't bother her? Did he want her to say she didn't mind being used?

The butler, thankfully, came in and set the flowers on the small table by the window. "I'll be back with refreshments," he said then hurried out of the room.

She wondered if the butler sensed the tension in the room. He looked happy to get out of there. She wished she could leave. Clearing her throat, she pulled the needle through the fabric, all too aware that Toby was watching her. Releasing her breath, she finally chose an answer that seemed to do the least amount of damage. "There's no sense in wishing for things that can't be. Neither one of us has the power to change the past."

She didn't look directly at him but sensed his frown. Whatever she said, she didn't think she could make the situation any better. Her anger had slightly abated, but the despair of knowing she wouldn't have the love match she craved had started to settle in, and that was harder to accept.

"I'm sorry, Toby. I can't pretend I'm happy with this," she finally whispered.

"I know. I don't expect you to pretend. I just want a chance to make it up to you, to prove I'm not the kind of gentleman you think I am."

Could she do such a thing? What he was asking her seemed like an impossible task, especially when the wounds were still too fresh.

The butler came in with a tray of tea and biscuits and set it on the table in front of them before he left.

She made another attempt to pull the thread through the fabric but pricked her finger. Gritting her teeth, she willed herself not to give away her discomfort. She didn't want Toby to pretend to be concerned about her. She rubbed her finger and thumb together and waited until the pain ebbed before she set the embroidery down.

Even if she wasn't thrilled to have him there, she should pour him the tea. "I have one request of you," she said.

"I'll do anything you want."

"Tell me the truth. Don't pretend to be something you aren't." She managed to get through the process of pouring tea without spilling it and handed him his cup. She left hers empty. There was no way she could drink anything right now, nor was she inclined to eat anything either. She motioned to the biscuits. "Help yourself."

Then she picked up her embroidery and started working on it again only because she needed something to do with her hands.

He held the cup but didn't drink the tea. Perhaps he was having trouble eating and drinking. He had mentioned something to that effect when he came in, but she couldn't remember the details. It was hard to focus when he was in the same room.

"Regina." He leaned closer to her, and she stabbed her finger with the needle again. "I promise you that I won't lie to you ever again. While I did make the wager with Lord Pennella, everything I said and did was who I really am." When she shook her head, he added, "I know it's going to take time to prove it. I don't expect you to believe me yet." He set the cup on the tray. "Thank you for seeing me. And for what it's worth, I am glad we're getting married." He stood up and bowed. "I'll see you tomorrow morning."

She watched as he left and almost wished he had stayed longer, but then she decided it was best he didn't. Short and to the point. At least it gave her a pleasant memory. They still had a long way to go, but at least it was a start. Feeling a bit better, she finally had a cup of tea.

Chapter Fourteen

The next morning, Regina stood before the vicar in church. A special license afforded them a faster waiting period. Originally, Regina had protested it, not eager to be married to Toby so quickly, which was ironic considering just a week ago, she'd wanted nothing more than to be his wife. But her father felt it best to get married quietly. This way, the affair was simple and small. And given the whole scandal, she couldn't fault his reasoning.

The whole wedding seemed like a blur. She mumbled through the vows, her heart hammering in her chest the whole time. Even if it was just her parents, Toby, and his friend Orlando, the room seemed to be closing in on her. Was she making the worst mistake of her life? Would she have been better off living as a spinster? She glanced at her mother who probably thought it was at least good she might have a son who would one day be an earl. But quite frankly, Regina had no idea how she could be with Toby that way.

Everything was happening much too fast. In some ways, it felt as if this was happening to someone else, and she was watching it all play out. She could barely be in the same room with him yesterday. How was she going to be in the same townhouse with him, let alone the same bed?

Though she hadn't felt up to it, her mother had insisted on the wedding breakfast, and given how small the whole affair was, there was no way she could run and hide. So when it came time to eat, she sat next to Toby. She forced down the food, not even tasting anything as she ate.

Her father seemed to be the only one who was having a good time. He rambled on about his business dealings with men who took ships of supplies from one country to another, seeking profit. "Such investments can be tricky," her father continued while eating his eggs with surprising gusto. "But I am a firm believer that the greater the risk, the bigger the reward. Nothing ventured, nothing gained is what I always tell my lovely wife and daughter."

Regina's mother politely smiled then sipped her drink. Regina, however, couldn't bring herself to even do that much. She was doing good not to bolt out the door and run off to a convent somewhere.

Her father swallowed some wine then added, "Of course, I don't put all my investments in one place. I might engage in a risk here and there, but I'm sensible, too. My wife would kill me if I wasn't."

Orlando laughed, and Toby joined in, though Regina sensed Toby was trying to appear relaxed when he really wasn't. His knuckles were white and his posture stiff, as if he was afraid of what was going to happen once they went to his townhouse. And Regina couldn't blame him. She shared the same apprehension.

"I always heard a wise gentleman listens to his wife," Orlando told her father.

"It's true. I listen to my darling flower often," her father replied.

Her father shot her mother a smile, and for the first time, it became clear to Regina that they actually loved each other.

"Most of the time, I spend my money in safe ventures," her father continued, either oblivious to the tension in the room or talking because of it. "I wanted to make sure my wife and daughter never had to want for anything. And," he turned his gaze to Toby, "I couldn't be happier that my daughter married so well."

Regina glanced at her mother who seemed as surprised as she felt that her father would come out and say such a thing. Maybe he saw something in Toby that neither she nor her mother did. But then, he was a gentleman, and maybe he thought wagers were perfectly fine, even ones with ladies who were stuck in the middle. Or maybe it was like her mother often told her: there was a secret code among gentlemen that said they had to stick together no matter what.

Toby at least had the sense to look shocked by her father's words, but he quickly recovered and murmured a thank you before he reached for his glass and drank from it.

"Oh, that reminds me," her father said, clapping his hands and shooting everyone an excited look. "I once invested money in a man who was going to Africa with a ship full of goods. To be honest, I had my doubts about him. He didn't seem like he knew the seas very well. But," he took another drink, "he knew his limitations. He didn't take unnecessary risks. I find the hardest gentlemen to invest in are those who think they know it all. Those are the ones you need to watch out for." He shook his fork at everyone and nodded, very satisfied with what he'd just said. "That's what's important, whether you are doing business or things of a more personal nature."

So that's what her father liked about Toby. Toby wasn't arrogant. And she supposed her father was right on that count. Even she didn't get that sense about him. It was something that had attracted her to him initially. But what about the rest of him? What was he really like? Unfortunately, only time would answer that question.

TOBY COULDN'T RECALL a time when he felt more helpless as he rode with Regina back to his townhouse. During the entire wedding, it had been obvious she didn't want to be there. Not that he could blame her. He was beginning to wish he had suggested they run off to Gretna Green. He had no idea that being surrounded by her parents and Orlando would make things even more awkward than they already were. But it had.

Between her mother's constant distrusting glances in his direction, Orlando's sympathetic smiles, and Regina's attempts to avoid eye contact whenever possible, the only saving grace had been her father who tried to smooth things over. He couldn't, of course. No one could make the whole process easier. But he had to admire her father for trying. His heart had been in the right place.

Toby looked over at Regina, hoping he could gauge her emotions so he could act appropriately. The last thing he wanted to do was step out of line. He cleared his throat and shifted, surprised when she jerked away from him, a startled look on her face. He paused. There was no doubt about it. He'd be spending the wedding night alone.

"I wasn't trying to get close to you," he explained. "I only wanted to get more comfortable."

She relaxed and nodded.

This wasn't a good sign of things to come. But he was determined to press through her wall. He'd managed to win her over once. Since he wasn't pretending to be someone he wasn't, he should be able to win her over again, even if it would take time.

"The wedding went better than I expected," he finally said.

She turned her gaze in his direction. "I thought it was awful. No one wanted to be there."

He wasn't sure how to respond to that because despite the circumstances, he had wanted to be there. Granted, it hadn't been the joyous affair he had envisioned when he proposed to her at Toplyn's ball, but he was still glad he married her. "Well," he ventured, "you didn't say no. That was what I was expecting. So from where I'm sitting, it didn't go as bad as I feared."

"Why would I say no? I already said I'd marry you."

"Nothing is final until the vows are spoken."

She seemed to consider his words for a minute then nodded. "I suppose you're right. I hadn't thought of it that way."

Her comment put him into a bit of a panic. She didn't believe she had the right to say no when the vicar asked if she really wanted to go through with the vows? If she had realized it, would she have said no?

He opened his mouth to ask but then decided he was better off not knowing.

The carriage finally pulled to a stop, and he breathed a sigh of relief. As much as he wanted to be close to her, he was glad for the reprieve from having to figure out something to say. So far, he'd been doing a horrible job of it anyway.

The footman opened the carriage door, and he waited for her to leave before he followed her. Though she didn't wait for him to walk with her up the steps, she didn't rush away from him either. That was the best he could hope for.

It was on the tip of his tongue to ask her to go to the drawing room and share some tea with him, but he was saved from having to risk her rejection when the butler approached him.

"This came for you while you were out, my lord," the butler said, handing him a missive.

Eyebrows furrowed, he took the envelope and saw it was from Pennella. Good heavens. Hadn't the gentleman done enough damage? Did he really need to keep hounding him?

"What is it?" Regina asked.

His initial response was to tell her it was from a gentleman at White's who probably wanted to speak to him, and while that was true, it wasn't exactly the whole truth. He studied her expression for a moment then directed his gaze to the envelope. "I'm not sure," he slowly replied. Who knew what Pennella wanted?

"Who's it from?" she asked, this time with a slight edge to her voice.

He had to tell her. There was no getting out of it. Thanking the butler, he gently took her by the elbow and led her to the drawing room. He shut the doors before facing her. "It's from Pennella."

As he feared, her countenance darkened. "What does he want?"

"I don't know." He didn't want to open the envelope. He wanted to tear it up and throw the contents away. Maybe he could even have the coachman drive over it with the carriage and send it back to Pennella to show him exactly what he thought of him. "Whatever it is, it won't be pleasant."

"I'm sure it won't," she muttered, crossing her arms.

This was just what he needed. His bride had been upset with him before the wedding, and this wasn't helping one single bit. "I haven't said anything to him since the day the wager was exposed in the *Tittle-tattle*," he told her. "And even then, all I said was that I didn't tell anyone about the wager and that I had no idea who did it."

Her eyebrows drew together, but she gestured to the envelope. "What does he want?"

"I don't want to know."

"Well, I do, especially since it probably involves me."

She was most likely right. "If that's the case, I really don't want to know. He's already gotten me into a great deal of trouble. Opening this will only make things worse."

"Then I'll open it." She held her hand out to him.

He cringed. "I can't have you do that."

"Why not?"

"Because it won't be good."

"Won't be good for you, you mean?"

"Yes. It won't be good for me. Or for you either. What do we need with Pennella anyway? He's an arrogant braggart who bullies people for the fun of it. I swear he lives for nothing else but to make people miserable." And he was doing a fine job of it, too.

She snatched the envelope away from him. "If it has nothing to do with me, then I will apologize and have nothing to say about him again. But if it does, I have the right to know."

It took all his willpower to remain still when all he wanted to do was snatch it away from her. "Please don't do this. Things are already tense between us. I don't want it to get worse."

She stiffened. "So it does have something to do with me."

"I don't know if it does or not, but..." After struggling to think of something he could say to convince her to put the envelope down, he gave up. "Whatever's in there, it won't be pleasant. It's never pleasant when it comes to Pennella."

Why he thought Pennella would cease to be a thorn in his side now that the wager was over with, he didn't know. Hope, he supposed. Dumb, naïve hope. With a sigh, he watched as she opened the envelope and pulled the letter out. As she silently read the contents, a scowl crossed her pretty face, and when she looked up at him, there was no denying the rage in her eyes.

"You made another wager?"

His jaw dropped. "No. I wouldn't make another wager with anyone after all this trouble."

"That's not what he said, and it's not what everyone at White's is saying either. My father is a fool for believing there's any sense of decency in you." She flung the letter toward him and stormed out of the room.

He wanted to run after her, but his gaze went to the piece of paper that floated through the air until it landed on the floor. He already knew he didn't want to read it, but like a horrible nightmare, he couldn't seem to resist picking the blasted thing up. Then he read it. His face grew hot, and he crumpled the paper in his hand.

Gritting his teeth, he stomped past a startled footman and butler without waiting for either one of them to open the front door so he could leave the townhouse. He was going to find Pennella and settle everything with him once and for all.

Chapter Fifteen

Toby flung the door open at White's and marched inside. Something in the back of his mind told him he should take a deep breath and calm down, but he just couldn't. Not when the words of Pennella's missive keep running through his head.

Congratulations on winning the latest wager. Miss Giles married you even after finding out about our little wager in the Tittletattle. I didn't think she would, but she was foolish enough to do it. Come to White's at your earliest convenience, and I'll pay you the money I owe you.

Toby's hand clenched the piece of paper as he looked for Pennella. When he found him lounging in the gaming room, he rushed over to him. And, before he could stop himself, he gave Pennella a swift punch in the jaw. Pennella flew backwards, tipping the chair over.

The whole thing happened so fast that he was barely aware of what he was doing. It hadn't been his intention to actually strike Pennella, but he was so angry, he couldn't think straight. All his attempts to repair the damage he'd done with Regina had been for nothing. One missive and Pennella upset the little progress he'd made. After this, who knew if Regina would ever give him another chance?

Before Toby could strike him again, Edon restrained him.

"What are you doing?" Edon demanded.

Roderick and Clement came over to them. "He's upset," Roderick told Edon. "And who can blame him? If it was me, I would have struck Pennella a long time ago." Roderick looked at Toby. "How you managed to restrain yourself for as long as you did is anyone's guess."

"Don't encourage him to do it again," Edon snapped.

Pennella rose to his feet and touched his jaw. "Don't worry. He didn't do any damage. I'm a little sore but that's all." He set the chair back by the gambling table. Then, as if to further provoke Toby, he smirked as he sat down. "You ought to take to fencing. Punching isn't your strength."

With a growl, Toby tried to hit Pennella again, but this time both Edon and Clement stopped him.

"Oh, let him do it," Roderick called out. "He'll do us all a favor."

"Stay out of this," Pennella barked, glaring at Roderick.

"I'm sure whatever you did, you deserve it," Roderick replied.

When Toby realized he was no match for both Edon and Clement, he stopped trying to get away from them. They waited a moment but finally let go of him, and Clement bent down to pick up his cane. The other gentlemen in the room remained silent as they watched Toby and Pennella.

Leaning back in his chair, Pennella directed his gaze to Toby. "You shouldn't be so upset, Davenport. I intend to make good on my word." He collected a few pounds from the table and held them out to him. "This will cover the wager I mentioned in the missive I sent you."

Toby waited for a moment to make sure neither Edon nor Clement would stop him before he crossed the distance to Pennella and slapped the money out of his hands. "There was no wager over whether or not she'd marry me."

The corner of Pennella's mouth turned upward. "I know."

Toplyn walked over to them and glanced at Pennella. "What's the meaning of this?"

"He's trying to make things difficult for Davenport," Roderick said. "Isn't it obvious?"

"It's true," Toby told Toplyn then looked at the other gentlemen. "He couldn't stand it because there was no winner in the wager we set, so he has to do everything possible to make me miserable."

Pennella snorted and crossed his legs as if he didn't have a care in the world. "I have no power over whether or not you're miserable. That is all your doing."

Toby shook his head. Pennella was enjoying every minute of this. If Toby punched him again, it'd probably make him laugh. Groaning, he began to rub his eyes when he realized he was still holding the paper in his fist. He smoothed the paper out and showed it to Edon and Clement. "See this? He sent this to my townhouse so my wife would see it as soon as we came home from the wedding."

"She saw it?" Pennella asked in interest. "I must say, you have more courage than I gave you credit for. I didn't think you'd dare let her read the contents."

"Go over there and tell her it's a lie," Toby demanded.

After a moment of seeming to consider it, he said, "Nah," and shook his head.

"You can't expect someone who has no morals to do the right thing," Roderick commented.

"Why don't you stay out of this?" Pennella asked him, turning an irritated scowl in his direction.

"Why can't you stay out of Davenport's marriage? It's bad enough you cornered him into that ridiculous wager. Be a grown gentleman and accept the fact that he got the lady instead of you."

Setting both feet on the floor, Pennella straightened in his chair. "No one knows who she was going to pick because you blabbed it to Gerard Addison at the *Tittletattle* before we found out."

"Are you still on that?"

"Are you still denying it was you?"

"Oh, stop it!" Clement interrupted. "It doesn't matter. The whole thing's been exposed. There's no undoing any of it."

"Of course, it could've been that ward of yours," Pennella told Clement. "Robinson is nothing but trouble." Then he looked at Edon. "Or it could've been you."

Edon shrugged. "I have better things to do than to worry about a stupid wager."

"He's right," Toplyn replied. "He has his father-in-law to contend with."

A round of laughter erupted, and some of the tension in the room eased.

Pennella gritted his teeth. "It had to be someone."

"Why do you care so much about who told some imbecile at the *Tittletattle* about the wager?" Toby demanded. "Are you really that concerned about your reputation with the ladies?" He threw his hands up in the air. "Fine. I'll come out and say it. You can get any lady you want. All you have to do is snap your fingers, and she'll come running. Before this whole thing was exposed, Miss Giles' mother was trying to secure a marriage between you and her daughter." As much as it pained him to say that, it was the truth, and maybe if he came out and said it, Pennella would be satisfied enough to leave him alone. "So you can see that if the wager had never been exposed, you would have won."

"That's not exactly what the wager was about," Toplyn argued. "It was about who Miss Giles wanted, not who her parents wanted."

Toby glared at Toplyn. Why couldn't he keep his mouth shut? "No, the specific agreement was the gentleman who got a yes to his proposal, won the bet."

"But it's implied she chooses the gentleman," Toplyn stated.

"Are you so worried about losing money that you'll press this issue? Since the wager was exposed, no one is losing or winning any money. All bets are off. What matters right now is saving Pennella's blasted pride." He gestured to Pennella who was still calmly sitting in front of him. "So, I am going to publicly do that right now." He turned to Pennella. "You are superior to me. You're better looking, you're more charming, you're more engaging. You are everything, and I am nothing. Does that satisfy you?"

Toby didn't intend for his voice to get louder as he spoke, but the words came out that way, and he couldn't seem to stop it. Right now, he was willing to do or say anything he needed to in order to get Pennella to leave him alone. And he was afraid Pennella had picked up on his desperation.

After a long agonizing moment, Pennella rose to his feet. "You have admitted that I won the wager in front of everyone. Despite what you said to Toplyn, that means I'm entitled to my winnings."

"You can't have Miss Giles. I married her this morning."

"I'm not talking about her. I'm talking about money. You promised me a sizable amount. An estate's worth, if I remember correctly."

Despite the grim situation, Toby laughed. He couldn't help it. All this time Pennella had been worried about the money? He hadn't cared a whit about Miss Giles or his reputation with charming ladies in general. It all had to do with money, and Toby had barely enough to rent a townhouse and hire a butler.

"What's so funny?" Pennella asked, glowering at him.

"There isn't going to be an exchange of money," Roderick spoke up. "The wager was brought to light before anything was publicly stated, and we're all witnesses to it."

"I agree," Clement added. "We won't allow you to take a single pound from Davenport, Pennella."

"Right," Toplyn quickly said, probably because he worried that he might have to give up his money to those who had bet that Pennella would win. He glanced at the other gentlemen in the room. "We won't let him do it, will we?"

The gentlemen shook their heads.

"This has gone far enough," the Duke of Ashbourne called out while the others murmured their agreement. "Pennella, stop this nonsense at once. You're acting like a child."

Pennella's jaw clenched then unclenched. "I'm going to figure out who told Gerard Addison about the wager, and when I do, I'll make him pay."

"Just let it be," Toby snapped. "We're all sick and tired of you bullying people." When he saw Pennella shake his head, he finally admitted what he had carefully concealed for years. "It doesn't matter. You're fighting for nothing. I don't have any money. I made the wager with you because I had nothing to lose. My father lost everything. I rent my townhouse, my estate is in need of repair, and I only have a butler. So all this letter writing," he gestured to the paper, "and all this talk of getting money is for nothing."

"Miss Giles has money, does she not?" Pennella asked.

Toby's jaw dropped. Was he serious? After all this, he still refused to leave the matter alone?

"This stops right now," Roderick barked and stepped between them, facing Pennella. "Miss Giles' money was never in the wager. You try to get anything from her and we'll have you thrown out of White's."

The other gentlemen agreed.

Toby supposed he should have received some satisfaction in knowing the gentlemen were supporting him, even despite what they'd just learned about his financial status, but he didn't. All he wanted was to be happy with Regina.

He wanted her to look at him the same way she'd looked at him that night at Toplyn's ball. She'd wanted to be with him, had chosen him, had risked a scandal just to tell him that she wished to marry him. She did all of that because she loved him. And if she loved him then, there had to be a way to gain her love again. But he couldn't do it while in London. Not with Pennella hovering about like a vulture, ready to take away any chance he had of being happy.

Toby had to get out of London. Even if his estate was in bad condition, taking Regina there was the best thing he could do for them, for their marriage. He shoved the missive at Pennella. "You can't control my wife."

"You can't control her either," Pennella replied, that irritating smirk back on his face.

"Unlike you, I have no desire to control anyone."

Without another look at him, Toby headed out of White's.

THAT EVENING, TOBY waited at the dining table for nearly an hour before he realized Regina wasn't going to come down to eat. He could only manage a few bites then gave up. He asked the butler to see to it that her portion of the meal be taken to her room.

Afterwards, he sat in the den, trying to think of what he could do to make things better. Pennella had him pinned into a corner, and worse, Toby had no idea if Pennella was finished or if he intended to do something else. He leaned back in his chair. He didn't know what to do. Nothing he'd say would convince her that he hadn't made a second wager with Pennella, and quite frankly, he wouldn't have believed it either if he were in her position.

Feeling as if the weight of the world was pressing on his shoulders, he left the room and trudged up the stairs that took him to his bedchamber. Her bedchamber was connected to his, and while he considered knocking on the door adjoining their rooms, he thought better of it and knocked on the door in the hall instead.

She opened the door, wearing a covering that hid her nightclothes from him. What he wouldn't give to see what was under there. But he wasn't welcome to her room. Not tonight. Possibly never. And before he could even open his mouth to speak, her countenance darkened.

"I hope you don't think something's going to happen between us tonight," she said.

Though her voice was tense, he noticed that she was struggling to be polite. Maybe that was a good sign. Or maybe not. It was hard to tell, and he was too exhausted to figure it out.

"No, I know nothing's going to happen," he assured her, slightly pained when she relaxed. "I just wanted to ask if you'd be willing to leave for the country estate tomorrow."

"You want to leave London?"

"I'm tired of all the things that have been happening. With Pennella. The wager and all. And the gossip. Aren't you tired of it?"

"My parents are here. They won't leave until September."

He cringed. Good heavens. He couldn't stay here that long, not with Pennella breathing down his neck.

She tapped the edge of the door then ventured, "What about leaving in August?"

Next month. It seemed like such a long time away, but he considered things from her perspective. Her parents were here in London, and after she left, she'd have to spend the entire autumn and winter with him. Those months were bound to be long and painful for her, unless he managed to convince her he was sorry about the first wager and had nothing to do with the second.

And she was willing to compromise with him. Instead of staying for two more months in London, she was willing to stay for one. The least he could do was meet her halfway. "All right," he agreed. "But will you please keep something in mind?"

Her eyebrows furrowed. "What's that?"

"I'm not making any more wagers. If Pennella writes another missive and claims I did, he's lying."

After a moment, she nodded. "I'll keep that in mind."

"Thank you."

Wishing him a good night, she softly closed the door.

He stood in the hallway for a good minute before he entered his bedchamber. With a heavy sigh, he took off his clothes in a slow and methodical manner. He draped them over a chair then blew out his candle and slipped into bed. He stared at the ceiling for a long time before he finally fell asleep.

Chapter Sixteen

When Regina woke up the next morning, she thought the wager had been a terrible nightmare. But as she took in her new surroundings, she remembered the *Tittletattle* and the wedding. She didn't know whether she should believe Toby or not about the missive Pennella sent yesterday. She wanted to believe him. It was bad enough he made the first wager. It made no sense that he'd do it again, unless he was so desperate for money, he'd do whatever he needed to in order to get it. But her father had already transferred her dowry to his account. Money shouldn't be an issue anymore.

She groaned and rolled over in the bed. It wasn't as comfortable as the one she was used to, but it was better than she thought it'd be, given Toby's lack of finances. Swallowing, she blinked back her tears. What if he had picked her because he heard her father was one of the wealthiest gentlemen in London? Maybe he wanted to get her father's money and Pennella's estate?

She'd be better off not thinking about it. She'd made a deal with him. In exchange for being a countess and possibly the mother of a future earl, he got her money. It wasn't a marriage based on love as she'd hoped. It was merely one of convenience. It was a secret bargain they'd made. No one had to know the details of why she agreed to marry him.

A knock at the door startled her. Toby wouldn't come in here this morning, would he? It'd surprised her he had knocked on her door last night. Though he hadn't asked to come to her bed, she wondered if that was what he was hoping for.

"Who's there?" she called out as she sat up.

"Milly, my lady," her lady's maid replied.

Relieved, she slipped out of bed and opened the door. Once she was in her morning dress and her hair was styled, she ventured down the stairs. She couldn't hide in her room all the time. She still had to go on living. At the very least, she could talk to her mother. What irony. She used to look for reasons not to talk to her mother, and now the prospect brought her surprising comfort. Maybe it was because her mother shared in her pain.

As she reached the drawing room, she saw Toby reading the paper. At least it wasn't the *Tittletattle*. She almost went past the room when he looked up and noticed her.

"Did you come down to eat?" he asked, hope in his voice.

"I did."

"Can I join you?"

She hesitated to say yes. She didn't want to eat in the same room with him, but servants were all over the place, and who knew if one of them was listening to them right now? After a moment, she consented. She waited for him to come over to her then followed his lead to where they'd be eating.

She collected her eggs, fruit and bread. Then she sat at the small table. She'd barely eaten the day before, and she was ready to eat everything in sight. But recalling her mother's rule that ladies should nibble instead of gulping food down, she managed small bites.

"I'm glad you're eating this morning," Toby said.

"Pardon?" she asked, wondering what would make him say such a silly thing.

"I heard you didn't eat anything for dinner, and I don't think you had much at the wedding breakfast."

With a shrug, she ate the portion of egg she'd had on her fork. "I didn't have an appetite yesterday." It was a difficult day to get through, probably the most difficult one she'd ever gone through up to this point in her life.

"I didn't have much of an appetite either," he softly replied.

She glanced at the butler and wondered just how much the servants knew. Did they know she and Toby hadn't consummated the marriage? Deciding she'd rather assume they didn't know the details of her and Toby's personal life, she concentrated on the food. If nothing else, Cook was good.

"What do you want to do today?" Toby asked after a long span of silence passed between them.

"I thought I'd pay my mother a visit." Noting the disappointment on his face, she asked, "Why?" He couldn't honestly expect her to spend the day with him.

"Nothing," he quickly replied, offering her a smile that she suspected was strained. "I just wondered."

"What will you do?" Perhaps go to White's and make another wager? She bit her tongue so she wouldn't say it. It wasn't fair. He might be telling her the truth. It was possible he hadn't bet on whether or not she'd actually marry him once the whole scandal was exposed.

"I don't know," he slowly replied. "I hadn't decided yet. Maybe I'll visit Orlando. See how he's doing since the lady he'd been hoping to marry decided to marry someone else."

She was about to ask which lady he referred to but decided against it. It was enough that they were exchanging pleasantries. Doing more would only expose her to being hurt in case she found out he was making more wagers at her expense.

Opting to forgo the conversation, she said, "I hope you'll have a pleasant visit," then finished the rest of her tea. She rose to her feet. "There's no need to stand," she said when he made a move to get up. "I'm restless this morning and need to see my mother right away."

Which wasn't the full truth. Yes, she was restless. But what she really needed was to get out of this townhouse. Because even now, she couldn't help but be pulled in by the sad look in his eyes. She'd been able to avoid them while she was preoccupied with eating. But now that her hunger was satisfied, she started to pick up on other things around her, especially the way he looked at her as if his entire world was crashing in around him and he didn't know what he could do about it.

Steeling herself, she left the room and went to her bedchamber to change. She couldn't afford to be weak. For all she knew, it was all a pretense to get her to open up to him again. She couldn't afford to do that until she knew she could trust him. And developing that trust was going to take time, if it ever happened at all.

If she kept catching him in lies, then she'd never be able to trust him. She tried not to consider that possibility as she walked over to her parents' townhouse. When she arrived, she was surprised to see Lady Seyton in the drawing room.

"Regina," her mother said as she jumped up from the settee and ran over to her. "How are you doing?"

To her shock, her mother hugged her. Actually hugged her. "I'm fine, Mother," Regina replied, tentatively hugging her back. She couldn't recall her mother showing such affection since she was a little girl.

"Come and sit with us," her mother encouraged, leading her to the settee and letting her take the spot next to Lady Seyton while she sat in a nearby chair. "Was your husband good to you last night?"

Regina's eyes grew wide then she glanced at Lady Seyton who was sipping her tea as if her mother hadn't just blurted out a very private question in front of her. "Mother, I'm sure we can discuss such things at another time." Preferably never. She'd rather dig a fork under her fingernail than talk to her mother about matters of a personal nature.

"I'm sorry. You're right." Her mother took out a handkerchief and dabbed her eyes. "I'm overcome with sorrow on your behalf. I don't know what I'm saying right now."

Well, that made sense. Regina relaxed. She could accept her mother this way as long as she knew it was temporary.

Lady Seyton set her cup on the tray and turned to Regina. "I hope you don't mind I stopped by. I wanted to see how your mother was holding up. I know she had her heart set on you marrying under better circumstances."

"That's very kind of you, Lady Seyton," Regina replied.

"I told you to call me Helena."

Though Regina nodded, she didn't know if she felt comfortable doing it, let alone thinking it, though she had the other day when she talked to her.

"Are you really all right?" Regina's mother asked, studying her face.

"I'm as good as I can be, all things considered," she assured her mother. "It's been a long week, but I managed to get a good night's rest and feel a little better this morning." She paused and listened for any sounds that might be coming from her father's den. "Is Father here?"

"No. He went to meet a business partner. Something about a ship ready to set sail."

That might be just as well. Her father was much too happy about the marriage, and she couldn't share in his enthusiasm. "I hope it proves profitable."

"These things often do. So," her mother poured her a cup of tea, "will you be staying in London now that you're married?"

Regina accepted the cup. "We discussed it, and we'll stay until August."

"Pardon me for intervening," Lady Seyton—Helena—spoke up, "but I overheard some rather unsettling things about Lord Pennella." She clasped her hands in her lap and slowly released her breath. "I've never had any dealings with him, but he's not known for being a gracious loser."

"You mean he wanted to marry Regina?" her mother asked.

"I don't know if he wanted to marry her or not. But from what I heard, there was a confrontation yesterday between your husband," Helena glanced at Regina, "and Lord Pennella. I wasn't given the details, but I heard the gentlemen at White's took your husband's side. Something like that won't sit well with Lord Pennella. I'm not sure staying in London would be best."

"Surely, Lord Pennella wouldn't do anything to harm either Toby or Regina," her mother said.

"Not physically," Helena replied. "But there are ways people can get revenge if they so desire."

Regina's eyebrows furrowed. Would sending a missive to a husband on his wedding day telling him he won a second wager constitute as revenge? Her hand tightened on the cup, and she bit her lower lip. It made sense. But was that the truth, or had Toby really made another wager? How she wished she could figure out what was really going on. If only there was something definite she could put her finger on. She closed her eyes and exhaled. All this thinking in circles was giving her a headache.

"Drink up, dear," her mother encouraged. To Helena, she explained, "Regina is apt to get headaches from time to time."

Regina opened her eyes and took a sip of the soothing liquid. It was a mixture of peppermint and green tea. Her mother often made that for her when she wasn't feeling well. She wondered if her mother knew she'd be coming by for a visit today.

Helena smiled and rested her hand on Regina's arm. "You need to do what's best for you, of course. No one can fault you for being upset." She rose to her feet. "Thank you for your hospitality," she told Regina's mother.

"You're welcome to stop in anytime," her mother replied.

Regina sipped more tea as her mother showed Helena to the door. Already the warm liquid was relaxing her, and she felt the beginning of her headache ease.

When her mother returned, she closed the door and sat on the settee. "Helena stopped by to give me my money back. She didn't feel right getting paid when it wasn't her lessons that helped you secure a husband."

"That was nice of her."

"Yes, it was." Leaning toward her, she asked in a softer voice, "Are you really all right, dear? Was last night horrible?"

Figuring her mother wouldn't relent until she answered, she finally decided to tell her what happened. "I didn't spend the night with Toby, nor did he insist on it. He only came to my bedchamber to ask if I'd leave London today, and I said no, that I wanted to spend at least one more month with you and Father."

Her mother breathed a sigh of relief. "Your father was so sure that Toby wouldn't touch you without your permission, but as a lady, I worried. Granted, your father's always been gentle with me, but I hear not all gentlemen are. Some even take what they want without caring one way or another what the lady wants." She dabbed her eyes again.

"I told you good news, so why are you still fighting back tears?"

"Because I misjudged Lord Pennella. Helena didn't just come over to give me the money back. She also wanted to assure me that you were much better off with Toby. Apparently, Lord Pennella wasn't the gentleman I esteemed him to be. I only hope that your father is right about Toby and that Toby will be good to you."

"I hope that, too," she whispered and finished the rest of her tea.

"I would like nothing more than for you to stay in London awhile longer."

Sensing there was more her mother wanted to say, she looked at her. "But?"

"Oh, I don't know." She wrapped the handkerchief around her fingers. "What if Helena's right? What if Lord Pennella tries to do something to come between you and Toby? What if he tries to make things worse?"

"How can he make things worse?"

After a moment, her mother shrugged. "I'm not sure. What I've learned long ago is that things can always get worse. Regina, this marriage might not have happened the way we wished, but now that you are married, I'd like for you to be as happy as possible. When your father and I married, it helped that we had the first few months of our marriage to be by ourselves. Maybe if you and Toby go to the country, things will get better."

"And if they don't?"

"Then you demand your own home. There's no reason why you have to live under the same roof as him."

Regina considered her mother's words and decided she had nothing to lose. "All right. I'll leave London."

Her mother hugged her again, this time openly crying.

"I thought you'd be happy I was doing this," Regina replied.

"I am, but I'm going to miss you. You'll always be my little girl, no matter how old you get or how many children you have."

"Mother, what is wrong with you?"

"Nothing's wrong, dear. I just want the best for you, and it's my fault you're stuck in this predicament. If I wasn't pushing you so hard to get married to a titled gentleman, you might be happily betrothed right now."

Regina put her arm around her mother's shoulders, touched her mother fretted so much over her happiness. "You did it because you love me. Neither one of us knew about the wager. We acted with what knowledge we had at the time."

"Can you forgive me for trying to push you toward Lord Pennella?"

Smiling, Regina squeezed her mother's shoulders. "Of course. I might not have been fond of him, but I had no idea he was as bad as he is."

And even now, Regina didn't know just how 'bad' bad really was. She only had an idea, but it was enough to make her grateful she wasn't married to him. Her mother embraced her, and Regina closed her eyes and hugged her back. For the first time in her life, Regina felt a close connection with her. The wager had changed things for the better between her and her mother. She could only hope she might one day say the same thing about her husband.

Chapter Seventeen

Toby stared out the window of the townhouse, wondering when Regina would return. She'd been gone for two hours now, and though she had married him yesterday, he wasn't sure she'd come back. He kept reminding himself that her clothes and other personal items were in her bedchamber upstairs. And it wasn't like she said anything about leaving. But he still found himself watching the clock in the drawing room and pacing the floor.

It was ridiculous, of course. He was acting like a lovesick school-aged boy, pining away for a lady's affections. He had never been in love before, and he didn't care much for how vulnerable it made him. When he first met her, he had no idea how important she'd become to him, but now that she'd lodged a place in his heart, he knew he could never love anyone else.

Catching a glimpse of a lady walking down the sidewalk, his heartbeat picked up, thinking it might be Regina. But it wasn't. He sighed and paced the room once more. She was coming back. She only went out to spend the day with her mother. It would be all right. He wasn't going to have one of those marriages where the wife lived in one place and the husband lived in another. They would live under the same roof.

She'd give him a chance to redeem himself. He hoped. Taking a deep breath to help settle his nerves, he returned to the window, praying he'd see her this time.

"My lord," his butler called from the doorway.

Toby jerked and spun around. After recovering from his shock, he relaxed. "Yes?"

"Lord Reddington is here to see you. Should I send him in?"

Good. Orlando would be a nice distraction while he waited for Regina to return. "Please do." He gave one last glance out the window then forced his gaze to his friend as he entered the room. "You want some brandy?"

Grimacing, he shook his head. "My head is still hurting from the memory of my hangover. I'll just have tea."

Toby asked the butler to bring them tea and waited for the gentleman to leave before saying, "You missed all the excitement at White's yesterday."

His lips curled up into a smile. "So I heard. Why don't you sit?"

"Oh, well..." Without meaning to, Toby looked out the window. Regina was still gone.

"She's not here?"

Knowing exactly who his friend meant, he shook his head. "No. She went to her mother's."

"That's understandable." He gestured to the chair across from him. "Sit down. Standing up won't make her come home any sooner."

Deciding his friend was right, he sat down but couldn't relax. "You don't think she's out looking for her own townhouse, do you?"

"It's possible."

"You were supposed to assure me that she's not doing such a thing."

Orlando's eyes widened innocently, and he shrugged. "But it is possible. Unlikely," he consented when Toby glared at him, "but possible."

"Some friend you are."

"What do you want me to say? That everything is going to work out?"

"Yes." Because he'd been praying all morning that would be the case.

"I don't know what's going to happen. If you'd told her about the wager from the beginning, this wouldn't be an issue right now."

"I couldn't do that. We made the wager at White's, and it was to be a secret for all the gentlemen there."

"While that's true, the secret could have been between you and her as well. There was no reason the rest of us had to know you told her."

"If I'd done that, I don't think she would have let me see her."

"There's no way of knowing if that's true or not because you can't go back in time and tell her."

Toby leaned forward and rubbed his forehead. "Why do you have to make so much sense?"

Laughing, he said, "It's easier to see things fairly when you're not involved."

"Unfortunately, that's true."

"All is not lost. At least she married you. There's still a chance you can turn this thing around."

Toby waited until the butler brought in their tea and left before speaking again, this time using a lower voice. "Pennella sent me a missive yesterday, and I received it as soon as she and I came home from the wedding breakfast."

Eyebrow arched, Orlando gestured for him to continue. "And?"

"Pennella said that I won the second wager and that I should come to White's to get my money."

"So that's why you struck him. I have to admit I'm impressed." Orlando picked up the teapot and poured tea into their cups. "I didn't think you had it in you. And I heard you got him pretty good."

"That's not the point. She was here when the butler gave me the missive."

"So?"

"So she thinks I made another wager with Pennella, except this time, I was betting that she'd be foolish enough to actually marry me."

Orlando stopped pouring the tea and studied him. "You didn't actually tell her the contents of that missive, did you?"

"I let her read it." When Orlando shook his head, he added, "After all the lying I did, telling her another one wasn't going to do me any favors."

"But telling her the truth about the missive didn't help things either."

"You're the one who told me to be honest with her from the beginning, to tell her Pennella and I had made a wager for the estates."

"Telling her that would have made sense." He finished pouring the tea and handed Toby his cup. "Letting her read the missive didn't."

"Either I'm going to be honest with her about everything from now on, or I'm not going to be honest at all," he snapped. Why did it seem that no matter what choice he made, he couldn't win?

"I'm sorry, Toby. I'm not trying to be harsh. I'm just saying that there are times when the truth works in your favor and times when it doesn't."

"If Gerard Addison hadn't reported the wager in the *Tittletattle*, it wouldn't even be an issue."

"True," Orlando consented then drank some of his tea.

Toby stared at the cup in his hands. The tea reminded him of that morning when he'd been having breakfast with Regina. He hadn't tasted it since he was so worried he might say or do something to make her run out of the room. And now, as he peered down at his cup, he didn't know if he'd ever enjoy tea again.

"You must love her," Orlando commented. "Even when you realized you had no money to your name, you didn't look so miserable."

"I'm faring no better than you did the night you found out Miss Boyle was getting married."

"At least it isn't too late for you." He took a drink of tea and softly said, "I envy you. Things may not look promising, but there's still hope. Once Miss Boyle got married, there was nothing else I could do."

Orlando had a point. He was married to Regina, and there was no way she could divorce him. But—he glanced out the window again—she could decide not to live with him.

"You want to know what I think?" Orlando asked as he set his cup on the tray and stood up.

"What?"

"That you might do well to leave London. Take Regina to the country. Get away from all the gossip. Don't let Pennella do something else."

Toby sighed and took a sip of tea. It was still too hot. How did Orlando drink it? "I promised Regina we'd stay here for another month. She wants to be near her parents for a while longer."

After a moment, Orlando nodded. "I can't blame her. And who knows? Maybe her father will talk her into thinking of you differently. He seemed to like you well enough at the wedding."

It was a small comfort, but his friend was right. Having her near her father might work in his favor...as long as there wasn't another rumor about a wager.

"Let me know when you get to Greenwood. I'd like to pay you a visit," Orlando said.

"I will."

As soon as Orlando left, Toby put the cup down and resumed his vigil by the window. He stood there for twenty minutes when he finally saw her walking down the sidewalk. She came back!

But before he could enjoy the knowledge that she hadn't stayed away forever, another horrible thought struck him. What if she was coming to get her things? His steps slowed on the way to the door of the drawing room. If that was the case, he'd rather not know.

The front door opened, and the footman greeted her.

"Where is Lord Davenport?" she asked.

Toby swallowed. She was looking for him? This was either good or bad, and considering how things had been going, he was afraid it would be bad.

"He's in the drawing room," the footman answered.

Toby quickly went to the bookshelf and grabbed a book. The last thing she needed to know was that he'd been waiting like a sad puppy for her to return. He leaned back in a chair and opened the book so he'd look as if he was reading.

As soon as he saw her enter the room, he lowered the book and straightened in the chair. "Did you have a good time?"

"It went better than I expected," she said as she removed her gloves.

"Oh?" Did she find another townhouse? He gritted his teeth so he wouldn't ask.

"Yes. It turns out my mother isn't the lady I thought she was."

She didn't mention another townhouse. That was good. But he wasn't sure where she was going with this. He closed the book and set it on his lap. "I'm glad you had a good visit. May I ask what you two discussed?"

He hoped she'd sit and talk. As it was, she was telling him more than she had in the past few days. If he could keep her talking, maybe they'd begin to work through the hurt he'd caused her.

She cleared her throat and tapped her foot on the floor. "While I was there, I made a decision."

Glancing from her foot to her hands, which were wringing the gloves, he gulped. This didn't look promising. She looked much too nervous, as if she had some unpleasant news to share and didn't know how to do it. He finally ventured a glance at her face and saw the resolute spark in her eyes. Whatever she decided, she was determined to follow through with it.

He braced himself for the worst. "What did you decide?"

"You were right. We should leave London."

At first, he wasn't sure he heard her right. "Pardon?"

"It's possible that you are telling me the truth about the missive Pennella sent yesterday, and if I'm to give you a fair chance, I need to get away from here. At your estate, Pennella won't have the opportunity to do something else." She made eye contact with him.

He blinked for several seconds, still trying to figure out what she was saying.

"Did you hear me?" she asked, her eyebrows furrowed as she studied him.

He stood up, clasping the book to his chest. "I'm sorry. I..." He dropped his book and tried to pick it up, but he couldn't seem to get a good grasp on it. Finally, he managed to retrieve it and offered her a hesitant smile. "I thought you were going to tell me that you wanted to live in another townhouse. I've been so worried that I haven't been in the right frame of mind."

She closed the gap between them and studied the title of the book. "I will accept that as a true statement. You were reading *A Lady's Guide to Etiquette*."

His gaze lowered to the book and heat rose to his face. Good heavens! The book must belong to the townhouse owner's wife. Not knowing what else to do—and trying not to die of embarrassment—he quickly put it back on the shelf. "I wasn't reading it. I...um...well, I just wanted to look like I was busy when you came in."

"Why?"

He winced. Did he really have to answer her question? He turned his gaze to her, hoping she wouldn't make him do it, but her gaze remained fixed on his, so he had no choice. Finally, he said, "I spent the morning waiting for you to return. I was afraid I wouldn't see you again."

"Oh." She paused for a moment. "The thought didn't occur to me. I knew I'd be coming back."

That was a relief.

"But," she continued, "I'm still not convinced you told me the truth about the missive from yesterday. Even so, I realize that Pennella is a problem. I'm not sure what kind of problem, but as long as we're in

London, he does have a way to come between us. I didn't marry him. I married you. I owe it to you to give you a chance."

"Thank you, Regina," he whispered.

She nodded. "I'd like you to get a better carriage than the one you currently have. I'm guessing the trip to your estate will take a couple days?"

"Two if we leave early in the morning."

"I prefer the ride to be as comfortable as possible."

"I understand, and I'll have a better carriage before the day is up."

"Thank you."

She turned and left the room. As soon as she was out of sight, he collapsed in the chair and breathed a huge sigh of relief. It was a start in the right direction. They still had a long way to go, but at least she was willing to give it a try. He couldn't ask her to do any more than that.

Chapter Eighteen

Regina woke from her slumber, surprised she had fallen asleep in the carriage. Even if it was the most comfortable one she'd ever been in, the swaying back and forth wasn't easy to get used to. She opened her eyes and saw the green pasture outside the small window. In the distance, she saw another carriage. She'd seen a couple others along the way on the well-traveled road, but she didn't think so many people would be out traveling in the middle of July. With a shrug, she straightened in her seat and worked the kinks out of her muscles the best she could, given the confines of the carriage.

It was well past noon, and they'd been traveling since that morning. This marked the first day of their journey to Toby's country estate. She supposed she should start thinking of it as her estate, too. She was the mistress of it, after all. But it would take time to adjust to her new life.

When she told Toby she wanted to leave London, she felt so confident that she was making the right decision. But now doubt started creeping in. Should she have stayed in London? Would it have made any difference?

With a glance at Toby, she saw he was sleeping. The book he'd been reading had fallen off his lap and onto the floor. This time he'd chosen to read something of a political nature. If she had to read something that boring, she'd fall asleep too, though to be fair, it was probably the tedious journey that got to him rather than the contents of the book.

She picked up the book and set it on the spot between them, accidentally touching his leg as she did so.

He stirred and straightened up. "What?"

"It's nothing. Go back to sleep."

It'd been the most they'd said to each other since she talked to him yesterday in the drawing room. It wasn't that she'd been avoiding him, but helping her lady's maid get her things together had taken the rest of the day, and they had left as soon as they ate that morning.

Now, as they traveled through the country, she had occupied her time with some embroidery while he read. Both were quiet activities that required no conversation, something that suited her just fine. She wasn't sure if she felt like talking to him yet. She had enjoyed her conversations with him in the past, but that was before she learned about the wager.

At the moment, she just wanted to do her embroidery and forget about everything. She needed to get to Greenwood. Once there, she'd take it one day at a time. She gathered the embroidery that she'd tucked in her valise and started working on it, taking comfort in the repetitive motion of pulling the thread through the fabric.

Several minutes passed before Toby broke the silence. "Do you enjoy doing that or are you doing it because there's nothing else to do?"

"I enjoy it," she replied. "It gives me something to work on, and it's soothing."

Hoping that would be the end of their conversation, she turned her attention back to it, but he asked, "What else do you like to do?"

Just as she feared, by waking him up, she had instigated a conversation with him. She should have been more careful with that book. "If you don't mind, riding in a carriage all day gives me a headache, and I have a hard time engaging in a conversation. Can we wait until dinner to have this discussion?"

Though he looked disappointed, he nodded and picked up his book.

She hadn't said it to be mean. She really did get a headache, and talking only made it worse. It was much easier to focus on what someone was saying when she wasn't bouncing around all day.

When it came time to give the horses another break, she went on a brief walk. Now she remembered why she dreaded the trips to London and back to the country. The long days in the carriage had a way of exhausting a person, which was ironic given all that she ever did was sit. The walk up the incline in the terrain was surprisingly invigorating, easing a lot of the tension in her body. She made it to the top of the incline and paused when she saw the same carriage in the distance she'd seen when she woke up from her nap.

Wasn't it odd that it stopped when hers did? Adjusting her hat to better block the sunlight from hitting her eyes, she tried to get a better look at the carriage. From where she stood, it was hard to make out the details of it, but she saw it had a darker color. It was either maroon or a rich brown shade.

But it wasn't in the best of shape. It was something a common gentleman might own. She bit her lower lip and thought over all the gentlemen her father knew who might own something like it, but she couldn't think of a single one.

"Are you ready to go?" Toby called out from behind her.

She turned and saw he was at the bottom of the incline. She considered asking him to take a look at the carriage but decided against it. It was silly, after all. What were the chances someone would actually be following them?

She could hear her mother saying, "Regina, you're so quick to assume the worst. Whoever's in that carriage is probably just tired and needed to take a break like we did. Let your imagination rest."

Regina gave one last good look at it before she turned back to her carriage.

When she reached Toby, he said, "We could stay for a while longer if you want to keep walking."

"No, I'm ready to leave."

Even if she couldn't explain why the carriage unnerved her, she knew better than to go against instinct. It was best that they leave.

The rest of their day was a quiet one, and despite her apprehension about possibly being in the same room with Toby, she was relieved to reach the inn. She wanted nothing more than to stretch out on the bed and close her eyes. After she put her embroidery back in the valise, she got out of the carriage. From the looks of it, Toby seemed equally relieved that their journey was over for the day.

Toby cupped her elbow with his hand and led her away from the carriage.

"Are you taking me for a walk?" she asked.

"No, but I will if you want me to," he replied.

"I'd rather eat." Now that they were out of the carriage—and would be for the rest of the night—she could think about food again. And her stomach was more than happy to remind her it'd been morning since she had a good meal. "What is it?"

"Would you like your own room?"

"I thought I made it clear we won't be sharing a bed, at least for a while."

Though he winced, he nodded. "You did."

"Then why did you ask?"

"Sometimes there's not enough rooms available. In case they only have one, I'll give it to you."

She hadn't considered that possibility, but she understood it might be the case. She also knew the stables or carriage would be an uncomfortable place to spend the night. "If that's the case, we'll share a room, but nothing will happen between us. Agreed?"

"That's fair. And thank you."

But as it turned out, his fears were for nothing. There were enough rooms available, and soon she was sitting in front of the vanity, brushing her hair. What she really wanted was a bath, but she could wait until they got to Greenwood.

A knock at the door interrupted her thoughts of soaking in a tub. With a sigh, she put the brush down and went to the door. "Who is it?" she called out.

No answer came, and Regina hesitated to open it. There was no telling who was on the other side. But something told her she should.

She retrieved a hatpin and held it behind her back. If someone on the other side intended to harm her, she'd use it. Granted, it was a feeble method of protecting herself, but it was all she had. With her free hand, she opened the door a crack and saw a lady who thought nothing of showing her cleavage to the world.

"Yes?" Regina asked.

The lady cleared her throat and spoke in a soft voice that required Regina to strain in order to hear her. "Lord Davenport asked for me."

Regina frowned. This lady worked here, and as much as Regina's mother tried to shelter her, Regina knew this lady did more than serve meals and clean rooms. She also offered her services to gentlemen. "If that's true, why are you at my door?" Regina asked, choosing her words carefully.

"This is Davenport's room. Isn't he here?"

"You were listening when the innkeeper gave us our rooms. You might have been hiding in the shadows, but I remember you." When the lady tried to bolt down the hall, Regina grabbed her arm and pulled her into the room. She shut the door and blocked the lady's exit. "What's going on? Why would you come here asking for my husband?"

Her lower lip trembled. "Please, my lady. I don't want any trouble."

"If you didn't want trouble, you shouldn't have come to my door and lie to me. My husband didn't send for you. Who did?"

"I didn't want to do it. But money's been tight."

"Someone paid you to come here and pretend my husband asked you to join him in bed?" When the lady started crying, Regina forced her tone to soften. She might not like any of this, but it was apparent the lady felt like she had no choice but to deceive her. "Who put you up to this?"

"I can't say. I promised not to speak his name."

Sighing, Regina went over to her vanity. After setting the hatpin down, she picked up her reticule and pulled out some money. Returning to her, she showed her the money. "I won't tell anyone you came here, but I do want to know who sent you and why."

Sniffing, the lady wiped her tears with the back of her hand and shook her head. "I don't know why. All I have is this." She pulled out a folded piece of paper from her pocket and gave it to Regina. "I can't read, so I don't know what it says. I was only told to give it to Lord Davenport."

Regina opened the paper with a glance at the lady in front of her. The lady didn't want to do this. That much was obvious. Her need for money must be great. Forcing her gaze to the paper, Regina read the note addressed to her husband, "No one makes a fool of me." It was signed by Lord Pennella.

"Where is this gentleman who sent you here?" Regina asked as she handed the lady the money.

"He's in his carriage."

"Can I see the carriage from my window?" Regina asked as she walked over to it.

"It's on this side of the inn, so yes, my lady."

Regina peered out the window, and her gaze went to the familiar carriage she'd seen a couple times earlier that day. "What does it look like?"

"A dark brown and reddish color."

Yes, that was the same carriage all right. So she hadn't been overreacting. And now she knew that leaving London hadn't stopped Lord Pennella from acting like a spoiled brat who was having a temper tantrum because he didn't get what he wanted. Well, there was only one way to put a stop to this nonsense, and Toby wasn't the one to do it.

Regina marched over to her door and opened it. “I want you to get the innkeeper to accompany me out to the carriage.”

The lady’s eyes grew wide. “You can’t mean to confront him.”

“Oh, that’s exactly what I’m going to do, but I’m not stupid enough to do it without some help.” Lord Pennella had just proven how underhanded he was, and she wasn’t about to face him alone.

Though the lady didn’t seem convinced this was the best course of action, she hurried out of the room and led Regina down the stairs to where the innkeeper was going through his ledger. As she explained what Regina wanted, Regina went to the window near the entrance and saw the carriage hadn’t budged. What was Lord Pennella waiting for? Did he want Toby to confront him?

Granted, she didn’t know Lord Pennella very well, so it was hard to figure out his motive. But if he was willing to run after her and Toby, she had no doubt he sent the missive on her wedding day in hopes that she’d be there to see it.

Gritting her teeth, she thought over what she was going to say to him. All he needed to know was that she caught him and knew exactly what was going on. Obviously, she was supposed to believe Toby wanted to take someone else to his bed. And she was supposed to believe that all Toby did was make wagers on how foolish she was.

The innkeeper came over to her. “I was told someone has been bothering you and you need my assistance.”

“Yes, that is correct. Will you escort me to that carriage over there?” She pointed to it.

He nodded.

“Thank you.”

Relieved he didn’t ask her why or suggest she have her husband escort her, she led him outside. She didn’t want Toby involved in any more of this nonsense. And if Lord Pennella saw her without him, it might make more of an impression on him. He wasn’t going to manipulate her like he had manipulated her husband.

She stormed up to the carriage and yanked the handle of the door before the coachman could open it for her. She got a wicked satisfaction in watching Lord Pennella jump in his seat.

"Is there something you wish to tell me, Lord Pennella?" she asked, her anger prompting her to exhibit a boldness that would have even made her mother run to another room.

He blanched, and she could tell he was struggling to come up with a sensible reply. Except, there wasn't one. She knew full well that he had no excuse. He was acting out of spite, trying to make things even more difficult for Toby. And even if she was still hurt from the wager, she couldn't accept someone treating Toby this way.

"I believe the silly wager you and my husband came up with is at an end," she said, her tone leaving no room for argument. "I know everything. I know you bet each other's estates. I know the wager fell apart the minute it was printed in the *Tittletattle*. I know you sent him the missive on my wedding day, and I know you lied about the second wager. I know you sent a lady to my room with the intention of making me believe my husband intends to share a bed with her. I know everything you've done and are doing. If you hope to make things difficult for me and my husband, it won't work."

She took a deep breath and stared at him, waiting to see if he would respond. But the fool only looked at her as if he was trying to figure out what was going on.

"I was going to choose Lord Davenport," she finally said. "You never had a chance, regardless of what my mother wanted. Even if I had to create a scandal or run off to Gretna Green to avoid a future with you, I would have done it. So you're much better off with things the way they are. This way you got to keep your estate." After a moment, she added, "You lost, my lord. Go home and deal with it."

She slammed the carriage door.

The innkeeper hurried after her. "My goodness, my lady, but that was mighty impressive."

"It was a long time in coming," she muttered as she entered the inn.

"My lady," the innkeeper said, jumping in front of her so she had to stop, "forgive me for being blunt, but I fancy a lady who isn't afraid to speak her mind. If there's anything I can do for you, let me know."

"Actually, I wouldn't mind a hot bath to calm my nerves."

"It will be my pleasure to have one brought up for you."

Since he was so obliging, she asked, "May I also have a cup of green tea with a hint of peppermint?"

"As my lady wishes, it shall be."

"Thank you."

She marched up the steps and headed down the hall. Her steps slowed outside Toby's room, but she continued on until she reached her room. She'd had enough excitement for the night. All she wanted to do was take a bath, eat dinner, sip her tea, and go to bed. She could deal with Toby tomorrow.

As soon as she entered her room, she went to the window and was satisfied when she saw Lord Pennella's carriage heading down the road, back in the direction of London.

Chapter Nineteen

The next morning after they ate, Toby led Regina to their carriage. Before she got in, he noticed she stopped for a moment and glanced around, as if looking for something.

"Is something wrong?" he asked.

After a moment, she shook her head. "No, nothing's wrong." Then she climbed into the carriage.

Wondering what she'd been looking for, he scanned the area but didn't see anything of interest. With a shrug, he settled into the seat beside her.

The carriage moved forward, and he spent the first hour staring out the window, not really seeing anything. He couldn't help but run through everything that had happened since that day at White's when Pennella came in bragging he could get any lady he wanted. Why did he keep torturing himself by thinking of all the things he should have done?

No matter how much he wished it, nothing was going to change the past. There was only one thing he didn't regret, and that was meeting Regina. He didn't think he would have gone up to her any other way. He'd been too afraid to go up to any lady because of his financial ruin.

He glanced at Regina who was staring out the window on her side of the carriage. He frowned. She seemed to be searching for something. "Did you forget something at the inn? Should we go back?"

She turned her gaze in his direction and shook her head. "No. Everything is all right."

Since she wasn't more forthcoming, he settled for nodding and picked up the very dull book he'd brought along for the trip. Most of the time, he stopped reading it and only stared down at it so she'd assume he was reading instead of thinking about her. If the wager had never been exposed, he thought they might have spent their time in the carriage kissing and holding each other. She might have even felt well enough to talk to him.

When the carriage came to a stop so they could take a break, he asked her if she wanted to take a brief stroll with him. He hadn't expected her to agree, but to his surprise, she did.

"A walk will help ease the stiff muscles," she explained, probably seeing the surprise on his face.

"Yes, it will." If that was why she agreed, he'd take it. At least she wasn't choosing to walk in another direction from him. "We should arrive at Greenwood right before dinner tonight."

She nodded. "I was going to ask you how much longer we have to go."

He wished she had asked. It would help him know what she wanted to talk about if she'd ask him something. He'd even be delighted to talk about something as simple as the clouds in the sky or birds flying in the air as long as he knew it would interest her. But she offered no questions, so he opted to tell her—or rather warn her—about Greenwood.

"I'm afraid Greenwood isn't exactly what you're used to," he began, even now resisting the urge to cringe as he remembered the way he'd left it.

"Is it a little cottage?" she asked.

It took him a moment to realize she'd offered a joke. With a smile, he said, "No. It's large. What I meant was that... Well, it's been years since it's been maintained. As soon as we married, I sent servants to fix it up so it would be deserving of you. But I'm afraid the poor staff will need longer than a couple days to restore it to its former glory."

"How bad is it?"

Her inquiry was made directly, and thankfully, there was no indication that she was disappointed. Maybe she had expected it. If that was the case, then he felt better already. "The lawn is overgrown, the stables show wear and tear, and the manor itself is in need of repair. Though," he added, "the inside needs it more than the outside. That should make the staff's job easier. And the furniture isn't so bad. I made sure to keep it covered to help preserve it. I also did it to protect it from dust."

She glanced at him, her eyebrows furrowed in that familiar cynical way of hers, which still had a tendency to endear her to him. Other gentlemen might have been put off by it, but he liked it.

"May I ask how your estate came into such poor condition?" she asked.

"My father wasn't a good businessman. And, he had a weakness for the gambling hells, especially when he got drunk."

"I hear a good number of titled gentlemen lose their fortunes that way."

"You heard right."

She stopped and turned to him, so he paused and looked at her. She had a way of looking at him with those amazing green eyes that made him want to hold her. And even more than that, he had the inclination to get on his knees and beg her to forgive him.

But before he gave into it, she asked, "When you and Lord Pennella picked me, was it because of my father's money?"

"No. I didn't realize you came from money until I came to your townhouse to take you to Hyde Park."

"Then why me?"

"You weren't easily given to flattery. Pennella relies on his charm to get his way with the ladies. I figured he wouldn't get away with it when he tried to charm you."

She smiled, and this time there was a hint of pleasure in her eyes. "Thank you, Toby. That's one of the nicest things anyone ever said to me."

He wanted to ask her why she said that, but the coachman called out that the horses were ready. It was enough they'd shared a pleasant moment. He wouldn't press his luck by saying anything else. He followed her to the carriage and got ready to continue their journey. This time when he opened the book, he didn't mind the silence so much.

THE NEXT MORNING, REGINA wrote a missive to her parents in the drawing room. When she was done, she decided to see what Toby was doing. He'd given her a quick tour of the place when they arrived the previous evening, but it'd been late. They'd only had enough energy to eat a quick dinner before retiring to their separate bedchambers.

Now, as she searched through the rooms, she wondered if Toby had decided to take a nap. While she'd gotten a good night's sleep, she was still a bit tired from their journey. But she knew she'd never be able to sleep right now.

She was ready to give up her search when she finally saw him in a room lined with portraits of his ancestors. She entered the room just as he took down one of the portraits off the wall to dust.

"Are you so bored you're wiping down the portraits?" she asked in a teasing tone.

He glanced at her and smiled. "I thought I'd make myself useful."

"There are a lot of rooms in this place. The maids will probably have more than enough to do for the entire winter."

"There's no doubt about it," he agreed and carefully wiped the cloth along the frame.

"How far back do these portraits go?"

"Six generations."

"That long?"

He nodded. "My family was a vain sort. They liked to see themselves as much as possible."

Chuckling at his joke, she closed the distance between them and looked at the woman in the portrait he was holding. "Well, I can see why. The lady in that portrait is beautiful."

"That was my mother. She was only eighteen when it was painted."

"She looked happy."

"She was."

Noting the hint of sorrow in his voice, she studied him. "She wasn't always that way?"

"She had a difficult time conceiving, and when she finally did, she had a difficult pregnancy. After I was born, she wasn't able to successfully have another child. I think the strain was too much for her, and she gave up on living. Then after that, my father took to drinking all the time, and the estate suffered for it."

"I'm sorry."

He turned his gaze to her, and despite the sadness in his eyes, she could tell that he'd made his peace with the situation years ago. "I don't want you to ever feel like you have to give me an heir and have a second son in case something happens to the first one."

So that was why his mother took the inability to have another child so hard. Recalling the conversation she'd shared with him the day they went to Hyde Park, she thought over his assurance that it wouldn't bother him if she had girls instead of boys. At the time, she hadn't been completely sure he meant it. But now she knew he had and, more importantly, she knew why.

Cupping his face with her hands, she kissed him. "Thank you. It is a lot of pressure to put on a lady."

"I know, which is why I don't want you to go through it."

She lowered her hands and found a clean cloth nearby. "Would you like some help getting these portraits cleaned up?"

"I thought you were writing a letter to your parents."

"I finished it."

"Already?"

"Well, I was in the drawing room for almost an hour."

"That long?" He dug the pocket watch out of his pocket and looked at the time. "I didn't realize it was so late."

"Time usually passes fast when you're busy," she said as she retrieved the cloth. "Mind if I help you?" She gestured to the other portraits.

"It's tedious, boring work."

"I don't mind. Besides, it'll give me a good chance to ask you about the people in them. I hope their stories aren't as sad as your mother's."

"Most are happier."

"That's good." She'd hate to think his entire family dealt with so much sorrow. "I know life isn't always nice, but I still like to think some good can be found in this world."

He placed his mother's portrait back on the wall and brought down the one next to it. "This is my grandmother. She used to write poetry and short stories for children. She'd read them to me when she came over. Hers was a happy story."

Regina took the portrait and chuckled. "You'd never know it since she isn't smiling."

"Yes, it's ironic. She looked so serious, but when you got to know her, you learned she liked to tell jokes and sing cheerful tunes."

"I suppose it goes to show there's more to a person than what you first see."

"I'd say that's a good way of putting it." He took down a portrait. This time, it was one of a gentleman. "My uncle," he explained. "My father's brother. Now, he was as dull as he looks in this picture. If he ever laughed, I don't remember it."

She chuckled. "You shouldn't say such things of those who are no longer alive."

"He's alive."

"He is?" She couldn't recall him mentioning a close relative before.

"He's in Asia. I'm not sure where. The last time he sent me correspondence, he said he was leaving India to go further east."

As she ran the cloth over the frame in front of her, she waited for him to continue but he didn't. She glanced over at him and saw he was dusting his uncle's portrait. "Well?" she asked.

"'Well' what?"

"What else did he write you?"

With a grin, he said, "He told me what the weather had been like, what he had hoped it would be like, and what he would have done about it if he had the ability to control it."

"That's all?"

"It was enough. The correspondence was ten pages long."

"Ten pages? And all he did was talk about the weather?"

"Yes. I'm not exaggerating."

"So, what did you write back?"

"Not much. I wished him luck on handling the heat in the summer and sent him a good hat to help keep the sun off his eyes."

Amused, she laughed.

"If I could have thought of anything else, I would have added it," he assured her, also laughing.

Still smiling, she brought her attention back to her portrait, careful as she brushed the dust off the lady's face.

"Regina?"

Surprised by the tenderness in his tone, she looked over at him.

"In the future," he began, "if our children or grandchildren look at your portrait, I want them to say your life was a happy one, and I'll do what I can to make that possible."

He turned back to the portrait he was working on. Though she was deeply touched by his words, she honestly didn't know how to respond. Deciding she didn't have to, she went back to her portrait and resumed her work.

THAT EVENING AFTER dinner, Regina waited until they were alone before asking, "May I take a look at the ledger? I'd like to see what the financial situation is, if you don't mind."

"You can see anything you wish," he replied then shot her an apprehensive glance. "My ledger is in my bedchamber. I put it there after we got here."

It made sense he'd keep it there. She should have expected it. But she hadn't, and the thought of being alone with him in his bedchamber caused a bit of anxiety to come over her. Forcing it aside, she said, "That's a sensible place to put it."

She went with him up the stairs and to his bedchamber. He lit the candelabra and held it up so she could get a better look in the dark room. Despite the awkwardness of the situation, she couldn't help but examine her surroundings. The rest of the manor was greatly influenced by those who had preceded him, but in here, she got a real sense of who he was.

The furniture in the entire manor was in good condition, as he had said, and his bedchamber was no exception. In this room, he chose dark oak furnishings with deep brown bedding. He had an armoire for his things, just as she did in her bedchamber. Then there was a full-length mirror, a lounging chair by the window, a place for his grooming supplies, a bookcase lined with books ranging from poetry and plays to full-length novels to historical accounts.

She was pleased that his tastes varied. It was nice to see he was willing to expand his knowledge. She always thought people who focused on only one thing missed out on what life had to offer.

"The ledger's in here," he told her as he headed for the small room.

She followed him and watched as he set the candelabra on the oak desk.

"I only have one chair in here," he said and opened the top drawer. He set the ledger down and gestured for her to sit. When she did, he asked, "Would you like me to leave?"

"I don't mind it if you're here while I look through it."

He nodded and remained in the room while she read through the accounts, mentally adding and subtracting the figures to make sure they all worked out as they should. He'd been careful to document everything he did for the past year, and she had no doubt he'd been just as meticulous with his money ever since he'd inherited the estate.

She glanced at him and saw he was looking out the open window. In the moonlight, he was even more attractive. She didn't know if that was because moonlight enhanced the way people looked or if it was the way her heartbeat picked up from simply being close to him. Regardless of the wager, she was still attracted to him. It wasn't easy to keep her distance.

But she couldn't afford to be vulnerable enough to get close to him. Not yet. But maybe soon, if he continued to be the gentleman he seemed to be.

Forcing her gaze off of him, she turned her attention back to the ledger. "You've been responsible with my father's money."

"I want to be. I know I have a long way to go, but I'm determined to do a better job than my father did."

"That's commendable." She closed the ledger and stood up. "I appreciate you letting me have a look at it. I don't think most gentlemen would be so obliging to the wishes of their wives."

"There's no reason why you shouldn't know what is happening with the money you provided me."

She stood at the desk for a long moment, not sure if she should say something or just go to her bedchamber. She had no intention of spending the night in here. He knew it as much as she did, but she still hesitated to leave, and she couldn't figure out why.

Finally, he asked, "Was there something else you wanted to see?"

Her cheeks grew warm, and she quickly shook her head. Surely, he'd been talking about the things pertaining to the estate, but her mind unwittingly went to the bed and the memory of the heated kiss they'd shared at Lord Toplyn's ball. He couldn't have feigned that kind of passion. At least, she didn't think he could. She knew she couldn't. Even now, her gaze went to his lips, and she thought there might be nothing better than to share another kiss.

Thankful the room was too dark for him to detect the blush in her face, she forced out, "No. It's been a long day. I should get to sleep. I'll see you in the morning."

Then, before she could talk herself out of it, she strode out of his bedchamber, choosing to use the door connecting their rooms. It wasn't until she closed the door softly behind her that she managed to breathe. Her back pressing against the door, she took a few moments to calm the beating of her heart. Once her swirling emotions settled, she walked further into her room and lit the candles so she could get ready for bed.

Chapter Twenty

The next morning as he finished breakfast, Toby ventured a look at Regina. She had managed to eat more today, which was a good sign. Maybe she was starting to trust him again.

Toby folded the napkin and placed it on the plate in front of him. The butler hurried to take the dishes out of his way, something that still seemed strange after all the years he'd carried his own dishes to the kitchen. Taking a deep breath, he looked at Regina again, noting the way she nibbled on a strawberry.

"I was thinking," he began, waiting until she looked up at him to continue, "it's a nice day out." He gestured to the large window where sunlight was streaming through it. After a moment, he cleared his throat. "Do you ride horses?"

She hesitated but swallowed the strawberry. "From time to time."

"Would you like to ride one today? I could show you the grounds."

For a moment, he thought she was going to say no, but then she nodded and wiped her mouth with a napkin. "I'll change and be down shortly."

Relieved, he rose to his feet. He was tempted to follow her but figured it was best if he didn't press his luck. Instead, he waited until she left the room before he proceeded to his bedchamber. Assuming this was going to be a pleasant ride, he decided to look forward to it. It was hard to be in constant dread that he'd do or say something to upset her. It was easier to focus on the fact that she was willing to spend the morning with him, and better yet, there'd be no servants around to overhear them. Sometimes he missed the privacy he'd enjoyed when he couldn't afford more than the butler. But he'd much rather be married to Regina and have the loss of privacy around him.

After the valet helped him into his riding outfit, he waited by the front door for her to come down the stairs. He wasn't sure what he was going to talk to her about. Maybe he'd tell her about the improvements being done to the place. But would something like that interest a lady? Would she rather he ask her what she'd like him to do to make the place more appealing to her? If she wanted a gazebo, he'd have it built. If she wanted a fountain, he'd get that done as well.

He heard her footsteps and turned in her direction. She wore the most attractive shade of green that accentuated her eyes. Her blonde hair was tucked under her hat. But more than that, her outfit brought out the curves he so desperately wanted to touch. He didn't know how it was possible, but she grew more and more beautiful every time he saw her. Could he tell her that, or would she assume he had ulterior motives? Perhaps she'd assume he was merely being polite.

Deciding he'd take the chance, he said, "You're beautiful."

She didn't answer right away, but when she reached him, she stood before him and thanked him.

All right, so she didn't peer up adoringly at him, but she did make eye contact with him and express her thanks. She didn't smile when she said it, but there was a softness in her voice that indicated she was making an effort. That was a step in the right direction, and right now, he'd take any break he could get.

The footman opened the door, and Toby led her outside. He wanted to keep his hand on the small of her back but quickly let go once they were already down the steps.

As they crossed the lawn to the stables, he asked, "Is there anything in particular you want to see?"

She glanced around the estate and shrugged. "Just show me the areas that most interest you."

He could do that. Maybe she'd like the stream that curved around the property. On some days, he'd even taken his boots off and dipped his feet in the water.

"All right," he finally said, deciding he'd start off by showing her the stream and let her take the lead from there. "But if you like a little mystery, I can always blindfold you and show you my favorite spot."

As he hoped, her lips curled up into a smile at his joke. "I didn't realize you carried a blindfold with you."

"Well, I have been known to wear one while riding a horse."

Her steps slowed and she stared at him, that familiar cynical look on her face, but this time, there was a hint of mischief in her eyes. "You blindfold yourself when you ride a horse?"

"Only three times, and it was a challenge."

"Was it?"

"Oh yes. Orlando didn't believe I could ride a horse with one on. But I've learned that by using a blindfold, I can judge where I'm at by the sounds around me, and the horse is never stupid enough to lead me right into a wall or off a cliff."

"You make it a habit of riding near walls and cliffs?"

Chuckling, he shook his head. "No, I don't. I was merely saying that my horse has too much sense to do something that foolish. The steed wants to live."

"I should hope so."

"So, if you want to, you can ride blindfolded, too. It's a good way to learn to trust your other senses. You'd be surprised at how much you can pick up when you're not relying on your eyes to tell you what's going on."

She shook her head. "You're probably right, but I'm not so..." She bit her lower lip and placed her hands behind her back.

"Foolish?" he filled in for her.

"I was thinking brave, but when I think of it, foolish works. Only a gentleman would wear a blindfold because he was dared to by a friend."

"It was all in good fun. Orlando was with me, and I knew he wouldn't let any harm come to me."

"In that case, it seems more of a testament to your friendship than an actual challenge."

"Gentlemen don't concern themselves with matters like friendship."

"They don't?" Her eyebrow rose in a way that indicated she didn't believe him.

"No. We're much too masculine for that kind of thing."

At that, she smirked. "Sure."

"How about you?" he asked as they walked into the stable. "You must have friends."

"Not anyone I would call a friend, but I've had plenty of acquaintances."

"No close friends?" he asked, unable to believe it.

She shrugged but smiled. "I had a childhood friend, but she got sick and died two years ago."

His smile faltered. "I'm sorry."

"I was, too, at first. But then I realized it was better to have been her friend and lost her than to have never been her friend at all."

The stable boy came over to them. "My lord and lady," he bowed, "should I get the horses ready?"

"Actually, I'll do it," Toby told him, encouraged that Regina was opening up to him. If he was able to keep speaking with her alone, maybe she would keep going. "Please leave us?"

He nodded and hurried out of the barn.

"You were telling me about your friend," Toby said. "Who was she?"

Regina turned to the horse and stroked its nose. "I don't want to bore you."

"You aren't boring me. I want to know."

After a long moment of silence, she said, "Her name was Judith, and we grew up together."

"Sounds like she was a good friend."

"She was. I don't endear many people to me. I've never cared much for large gatherings, and it's hard for me to open myself up to people."

"I figured as much."

She glanced at him then turned her attention back to the horse. "Anyway, she was the only one who continued to come by and visit with me. I still can't figure out why. There wasn't much I'd say when she was around. It wasn't that I didn't think of things to say. I was just afraid she'd think whatever I said was silly and not want to come around anymore."

"So you wanted her to visit?"

"I did, but I didn't want to tell her. I ended up telling her years later after I was comfortable enough to know she wouldn't run off and find someone else to spend time with. We were supposed to go through our Season together, have our weddings together, and raise our children together."

Her voice broke, and she edged away from him and stroked the horse's neck.

"I haven't known that kind of loss," he said, his voice soft.

He stepped closer to her, and though she tried to step away from him, the stall door prevented her from doing so. Realizing he'd made her uncomfortable, he eased back a bit to give her more space, and she relaxed.

"It sounds like she was a good friend, and it sounds like you closed yourself off from the rest of the world after she died." It made sense, and it probably explained her skepticism when it came to new people. "You don't make friends easily, do you?"

"I don't need the kind of friends who end up having fun at my expense behind my back."

At first he thought she meant him, but then it dawned on him that she was thinking of her past, specifically to a time in her childhood when she thought those other girls were her friends but had overheard them making fun of her. And if he guessed right, Judith hadn't done that to her.

"I'm glad you had someone like Judith in your life," he finally said, knowing that she wouldn't believe him if he told her he never wanted to hurt her by agreeing to the stupid wager. It'd never been his intent to make her the object of a joke, but he could see how she'd think that and couldn't fault her for reacting the way she did. "Thank you for telling me about her."

Her gaze met his, and he saw the unshed tears in her eyes as she blinked them away. "I always thought if I had a girl, I'd name her after her."

"We can do that," he whispered.

Noting the spark of hope in her eyes, he gently brought his finger under her chin and tilted her head back so he could get a better look at her. She wasn't trying to get away from him. In fact, she was still looking at him, and better yet, the wall she'd erected to keep him out had faded. She had finally let him in.

Sensing the moment was right, he brought his lips to hers. How he missed the softness of her lips and the way she sighed in pleasure when he traced his tongue along the seam of her lower lip.

But just as soon as she seemed to be opening up to him, she pulled away. She didn't say anything for a long time as she ran her hand down the horse's neck, and he wasn't sure if he should apologize or act like the kiss never happened.

"I'm sorry," she finally said, startling him.

"What do you have to be sorry for?" She wasn't the one who stepped out of line and kissed him.

"I'm trying to forgive you for the wager, but it's hard."

"I know. If the situation was reversed, I'd have a hard time of it, too."

After a moment, she turned back to him. "I do believe you about the missive Lord Pennella sent you on our wedding day."

"You do?" he asked, afraid he hadn't heard her right. She had no reason to believe him, none that he could see anyway.

"I do. I may not know much about Lord Pennella, but he is the type of gentleman who'd do something like that. I get the impression he doesn't want others to be happy."

Maybe. Maybe not. All he knew about Pennella was that he liked to boast about how wonderful he was, and that often included putting others down. "I try to avoid him whenever I can. It's just that White's isn't that big. You can't help but run into someone if they want to find you."

"It seems to me all of London is that way. No matter where I went, I used to end up seeing the same group of people after awhile."

He nodded, and she backed away from the horse.

"I'll let you saddle the horses."

He quietly worked through the process, and as he was finishing up with the second horse, she cleared her throat. Glancing over at her, he asked, "Have you changed your mind about riding?"

"No, I..." With a shy smile, she shook her head. "Never mind."

"What is it?"

She bit her lower lip as she wrapped the reins of her horse around her hand. "I couldn't help but notice that you're adept at this thing. With the saddle and all. I don't know the first thing about it."

"Do you want me to show you?"

"No. I have no interest in learning how to do it. I just wondered how you got to be so good at it."

"Remember what I told you about doing as much as servants do?" When she nodded, he added, "This was one of the things I learned.

Riding this horse was one of the few enjoyable things I had to do out here." He patted its neck affectionately.

Her smile widened. "That's nice."

"For what it's worth, I like spending time with you more than I do riding a horse."

His horse snorted in protest.

Laughing, he stroked its neck again. "I'm sorry, but it's true."

"Then it's good that we'll go horseback riding together. You can have two things you enjoy," she replied.

Pleased, he grinned. "It'll make for a most enjoyable morning."

Once they were on their horses, he led her out of the stable and down the path that would take them to the stream. The tension between them had subsided, and in its place was a flicker of the warm companionship he had experienced with her before she discovered the wager. Maybe there was hope. Maybe there would be more kisses. More laughter. And maybe there would even be children. Even if they only had girls, he'd be happy. All he wanted was for her to look at him the same way she had that night at Toplyn's ball. If he could get that again, he'd die a happy gentleman.

He slowed so she could come up beside him.

"You have a good view out here," she said.

Forcing his gaze off of her, he noted the land surrounding them. Trees lined parts of the property, but mostly the flat landscape was covered in tall grass. "There's a stream down that way." He gestured to the left. "I thought we might go there."

"All right."

They rode on in a comfortable silence, and when they reached the stream, he helped her down from the horse.

"I used to come down here a lot when I was younger," he told her as he secured the horses' reins to the trees.

"Did you?"

"Yes, especially when I was a boy. Orlando and I would come here and swim."

Her eyebrow raised, she asked, "In a shallow stream?"

"I didn't say we were successful at it."

As he hoped, she chuckled. "I suppose being children, you two were pretending to swim."

"Yes. But as I got older, I still liked to come down and take off my boots so I could enjoy the cold water. It was especially refreshing on a hot day like this. What do you say? Want to go in without your boots on?"

"And get my stockings wet?"

"Just take them off."

She gasped, her green eyes growing wide. "I can't do that. Not outside the bedchamber."

"Why not?" He glanced around. "No one can see you. The manor is a good mile away, and we're surrounded by trees."

Her face turned pink. "I just can't. I wish to remain fully clothed during this outing."

"I'll tell you what. I'll go in first."

As he slipped out of his boots, she asked, "You're not going to go in there without taking off your stockings, are you?"

"I don't wear stockings," he replied. "But I will keep my drawers on." He motioned to his footed-drawers. "I'd have to remove my breeches in order to take them off."

"Oh."

Amused, he teased, "I wouldn't be opposed to doing that if wet drawers bother you."

"No. I mean, you need to keep them on. What if," she glanced around, "someone sees you?"

"No one but you will see me." To save her from having to reply, he stepped down into the stream, careful as he stepped over some rocks.

Turning back to her, he called out, "It feels great. Are you sure you don't want to join me? We can sit on that large rock over there."

Though she followed his gaze, she shook her head. "I can't."

"Why not?"

She shrugged. "I just can't."

"All right." He wouldn't push her. If she wasn't comfortable, she shouldn't have to do it. But it wasn't much fun standing in the middle of the stream all by himself. So he only stayed there long enough to pick up a couple purple and white flowers growing along the grassy edge and returned to her. "These are for you."

"They're beautiful." She accepted them and smelled them. "They have a pleasant fragrance."

"I'm glad you like them." With a smile, he slipped his boots back on.

"Is it uncomfortable to wear those when your...drawers...are wet?"

"Only a little, but I do feel much cooler."

They went to their horses and rode back to the stables. Deep down, he believed everything was going to be all right.

Chapter Twenty-One

The next day, Regina stood by the stream. She made sure the manor was far away enough so that no one would see her. It was silly to worry, she supposed. No one had been the wiser when Toby stepped into the stream. She had been curious about what it would be like to feel the cool water on her feet. Toby seemed to enjoy it, and while he'd been out there, she had to hold back the urge to free herself of her inhibitions and join him.

With another glance around to make sure no one was nearby, she slipped out of her riding boots then removed her stockings. She lifted the hem of her riding skirt and petticoats. Her heartbeat picked up in excitement as she stepped on the grass. She'd never exposed so much of herself in public in her entire life. Granted, no one was there to see her, but the possibility someone might was enough. Taking a deep breath, she edged closer to the stream. The area was muddy, given last night's storm, so she tried to be careful as she proceeded forward.

But as she stepped down toward the stream, she tripped on a tree root and lost her balance. Letting out a shriek, she let go of her skirt, her arms flailing in front of her in the most ridiculous fashion as she tried to find something—anything—to grab onto. But her efforts were in vain, and she only grasped a handful of mud on her way down into the water.

She landed face first in the cold stream. The whole thing happened so fast, she couldn't even describe it to anyone who asked. But she ended up drenched from head to toe, mud clinging to her and blood seeping from her sleeve. Wincing, she sat up and peeled back her sleeve to see how badly she'd injured her arm. Relieved, she sighed. Good. It was just a gash. Her sleeve had suffered the brunt of it. She'd never be able to wear this riding outfit again.

She stood up and pushed the hair out of her eyes then picked up the hat, which was lying a few feet from her. Well, so much for dipping her feet in. She trudged back onto the grass and put her stockings and boots on. Though she was sore, she'd survive. Her biggest angst was being embarrassed when the others saw her.

Reminding herself she was much better off getting dirty than breaking a bone, she rode to the stables.

"My lady," the startled stable boy said as he helped her dismount. "What happened?"

"N-nothing," she mumbled through chattering teeth.

She hadn't thought it possible on a nice summer day, but in her wet clothes, she experienced a chill. After she handed him the reins, she headed for the house, her skirt clinging to her legs, making it difficult to go as fast as she desired. When she finally made it to the steps of the front door, she breathed a sigh of relief. She'd made it. The trek back from the stream seemed like the longest one she'd ever had to take.

The footman opened the door, his jaw dropping at the sight of her.

"I had an accident in the stream," she said.

Before he could say anything, she headed for the staircase.

"My lady," the butler called out as he hurried toward her. "Shall I have a bath drawn for you?" His gaze went to the blood soaking the sleeve of her dress. "And send someone to tend to your injury?"

"It's only a scratch," she assured him as she slowly climbed the stairs. Her legs were bruised by the feel of it. "And yes, a bath would be nice."

"I'll have a bath sent up immediately."

She thanked him and continued up the staircase. What a sight she must have made, what with the mud clinging to her and all. If she'd gone with Toby, she supposed none of this would have happened.

By the time she reached her bedchamber, she was shivering. She shut the door and started removing her clothes. Once she got out of them, she'd feel a lot better. There was a knock at her door. Figuring it was her lady's maid, she called out, "Enter," and slipped out of the last of her things as the door opened and closed.

"I heard you were hurt," came a familiar voice that definitely didn't belong to her lady's maid.

Gasping, she looked up and saw Toby. She made a futile attempt to cover herself. Why didn't she think to go behind the dressing screen?

He headed over to her. "You're bleeding."

"It's nothing," she said and hurried behind the screen.

But he followed her. "It's not nothing. You're dripping blood on the floor."

She groaned when she realized he wasn't going to leave her alone. "It's a gash, nothing more." She held her wounded arm out to him while doing her best to cover herself with her other arm, and that really didn't do much good.

He gently took her arm and studied the long gash that ran from her elbow down to the middle of her arm. Dabbing the blood away with the sleeve of his shirt, he released his breath. "You're right. It's not as bad as it looks."

"No, it's not. Now can I have my arm back?"

"Oh, of course."

She took the opportunity to try to conceal more of herself. When there was a knock at the door, she said, "That's probably my bath."

"I'll have them bring it in."

Before she could argue that she wanted him to get out of there so she could bathe in private, he was already at the door and telling the servants where to put the tub. She even overheard him telling her lady's maid that he was going to take care of her. Her eyes grew wide. What was he doing? It wasn't his place to wash her or help her with her clothes. But she couldn't speak up and protest, not when the servants were on the other side of the screen.

After the servants shuffled out of the room, he peered around the screen and waved her forward. "It's all right. There's no one here."

"You're here," she managed to squeak. She cleared her throat, mentally cursing herself for giving away her apprehension.

"I'm going to help you wash the mud out of your hair and tend to that arm." His gaze lowered. "Did you hurt your legs?"

"Bruises," she muttered and hurried past him so she could get into the tub.

She'd been standing naked in front of him long enough, and even though she did her best to hide her breasts and the other notable part of her body from him, she didn't think she was doing that great of a job. She slipped into the tub and winced. The hot water was enough to sting her skin, but she would rather risk getting red than remain naked in front of him.

"The maids brought in soap and towels," he said, though she thought it unnecessary since they did that every time she took a bath. "They also brought bandages to put on your wound if necessary."

She nodded and got as comfortable as she could in the tub. She took a deep breath and brought her legs up to her chest. There. That was better. Now he couldn't see so much of her. When she dared a glance over at him, he was rolling up the sleeves of his shirt.

He picked up the bar of soap and dipped it in the water. He grimaced and shook his hand. "How can you stand water that hot?"

With a shrug, she muttered, "I was cold."

"I suppose. You'd have to be to sit in water this hot. I'll look for a comb so I can take care of your hair."

Her eyebrows furrowed. Didn't he realize she was naked? He didn't seem to be trying to peek at her body. Maybe he was so concerned about her that he wasn't paying attention to what was really going on.

"Is this comb good?" He lifted one of her combs from the vanity and showed it to her.

After a moment, she nodded. All right. So he wasn't fully aware of what was going on. Either that, or he had no interest in seeing her naked, something she didn't think possible after that kiss they'd shared at Lord Topylin's ball. Even now the memory made her skin flush.

He brought the comb over to the small table by the tub and set it next to the towels. "Can I wash your arm?"

She held her arm out, and he knelt by the tub. He picked up the cloth and dipped it into the water. Then he lightly brushed it over her wound. She sharply inhaled. It might not have been a deep wound, but it still stung.

"I'm sorry. I'll be as gentle as I can," he said then dabbed the water along the length of her injury.

She bit down on her tongue. When he washed it with soap, it was worse. But then he rinsed it off by pouring water from a small bowl on it, and she relaxed.

"Good. It looks like the bleeding is slowing down," he commented.

He let go of her arm then knelt behind her. He took the pins out of her hair and set them on the table.

"I didn't realize you were so adept at removing pins from a lady's hair," she joked.

He chuckled. "They're easy enough to remove, though," he added as he set the last pin aside, "I can't say I've ever done this before. You're the first."

Surprised, she glanced back at him as her damp hair tumbled over her shoulders. "Am I the first lady you've bathed?"

He had been reaching for the soap in the tub when she made the inquiry, and judging by the way he grew still, she figured it finally dawned on him that she was naked.

Despite herself, she chuckled. "Next, you're going to tell me you've never been with a lady who had no clothes on."

His face grew red while he pulled the soap out of the tub. "I haven't, actually."

She studied him to determine if he was telling her the truth or not and finally decided he was. The realization pleased her. She hadn't thought any of the gentlemen chose to go without a dalliance of some sort before marriage, and it was nice to know he had.

She remained quiet as he rinsed her hair before washing it with soap. Then he rinsed it off again. He took his time in combing her hair, careful as he worked through her tangles. It was a very soothing action, and she found herself relaxing more and more with each passing minute.

"Thank you," she finally said.

"All I'm doing is combing your hair."

"I know, but it's the way you're doing it. You're being tender." She cleared her throat. "You were tender when you cleaned the wound on my arm, too."

"Oh," he replied, sounding a bit shy.

This was the same gentleman she saw standing in the drawing room of her parents' townhouse, practicing different ways to ask her if she was going to attend Lord Toplyn's ball. He'd been unsure of himself, questioning what he was saying and how he was saying it. She'd found it so endearing. Since finding out about the wager, she thought he'd only been practicing what to say because he wanted to make sure she didn't spend much time with Lord Pennella. But maybe it'd been as she first thought, that he had sincerely cared about her.

He had no reason to pretend to be someone he wasn't now that he was married to her. He didn't have to tend to her wound and wash her up, but he was choosing to do that. And in none of his movements did he indicate that he planned to take her to bed.

When he was done with her hair, he cleared his throat and stood up. "I'll tell your lady's maid to come in to help you get dressed for dinner."

"You're leaving?"

He stopped halfway to the door and turned toward her. "I wanted to make sure you were all right and help you get that mud out of your hair. I figure you can do the rest yourself, and your lady's maid knows how to help you with your clothes."

Noting the way he shifted from one foot to the other, she offered him a reassuring smile. "Well, I can't wash my back, and I'd rather not have my lady's maid do it for me."

He hesitated, as if he didn't understand her meaning.

Realizing he needed a little more encouragement, she picked up the soap and held it out to him, sitting up straighter so her legs were no longer hiding her breasts. As she expected, his gaze went to them. Blushing, he quickly brought his eyes back up.

"You want me to wash your back?" he asked, the same uncertain expression on his face that he'd had before she found out about the wager.

"If you don't mind?"

"No, I don't mind," he softly replied.

He walked back over to her, took the soap, and knelt behind her. She pulled her hair over her shoulder. She chanced a glance at him and saw the same gentleman she'd fallen in love with. This was the gentleman who'd made her feel as if what she thought mattered. The others had been so preoccupied with themselves, more concerned about what they could get from her instead of learning about who she was. But Toby had been different. He'd taken an interest in her. Maybe it hadn't been an act. Maybe he had been sincere the whole time.

He washed her back, and it took her a moment to realize his hands were trembling. It was subtle but still noticeable.

"You have no need to be afraid," she said. "I won't bite."

He let out an uneasy chuckle. "I didn't say I thought you would."

"No, but I can see that you're not comfortable around me." She cleared her throat. "I want you here."

"Are you sure?"

"I wouldn't have said it if I didn't mean it."

"Well, I...I suppose not."

As he continued washing her back, she ventured, "Can I ask you something?"

"Of course."

"I want you to tell me the truth."

He didn't answer right away but finally said, "I've been telling you the truth ever since you found out about the wager in the *Tittletattle*. I'll do the same now."

She nodded. "Did you care for me those times when you came to visit?"

"Yes," he whispered. "From the first time I danced with you, I cared about you."

"Really?"

"Really." He leaned forward and kissed her shoulder, and this time when she shivered, it was from the thrill of having his lips touch her skin. "I was impressed by your wit."

"Wit? All I did was complain about everyone attending the ball."

He laughed. "I know, but it was an honest observation." He continued washing her back and added, "I was just as guilty as everyone else. You were probably the only honest person in the entire place."

She turned around as much as the tub would let her so she could get a good look at him. "You liked me from the first time we met?"

"I did. Out of all the ladies there, I saw something in you I didn't see with anyone else. I saw a future. I didn't plan for it, but as soon as I realized the possibility was there, I wanted to spend more time with you. I couldn't do that while pretending to be interested in someone else for the sake of the wager." He reached for her hand and brought it to his lips. "I'm sorry. Orlando said I should've been honest with you from the beginning, but I was afraid if I was, you wouldn't want to have anything to do with me."

"You were right. I wouldn't. But then, I wouldn't be here now."

His eyes met hers, and since he didn't seem to understand her meaning, she cupped the back of his neck and pulled him toward her so she could kiss him.

She thought he might hesitate to kiss her again since there was that hint of uncertainty in his reaction to her kiss. But then he relaxed, slipped his arms around her, and brought his lips back to hers. The kiss was just as exciting as the others they'd shared. Before her Season, she had assumed kissing would be pleasant enough, but she had no idea it could make her tingle from the top of her head straight down to the tips of her toes.

His tongue traced her lower lip, and she parted her mouth to accept him. Up to now, this was about as far as they'd gone, with the exception of him touching her breasts, of course. But she knew this time, they would go even further than that. Maybe it was a wager that led him to her, but it wasn't what connected them. Her feelings had, indeed, been reciprocated all along.

When the kiss ended, he pulled away from her, not seeming to mind the fact that most of his shirt was wet. Picking up the soap, he worked up a good lather and said, "I thought since you started a bath, you should finish it." He gestured to her arm. "How are you doing?"

She examined it and saw that the bleeding had stopped. "I'm fine. I'm surprised there was so much blood to begin with."

"You must've hit the rocks and tree branches just right, so it looked worse than it was." He ran his soapy hand down her arm. "What were you doing at the stream anyway?"

"Enjoying the day. I thought it was a pretty place when you showed it to me. And," she cleared her throat, "I was curious about dipping my bare feet into the water."

Eyebrow raised, he glanced at her. "You were?"

She nodded.

"Why didn't you do that when I was with you?"

"Because it seemed silly at the time. But then I thought that there had to be some appeal to it if you liked it."

"Next time I'll go with you, so we can do it together. And," he added as he traced one of her legs with the bar of soap, "I'll hold you so you don't slip."

She chuckled. "Given my grace, I'll need the help."

He grinned. "You have grace. I saw you dance. You handled yourself very well on the dance floor."

"Only because my mother insisted I attend endless lessons."

"Her persistence paid off." He lifted her leg so he could wash her foot. "Is your leg sore?"

"Not at the moment." In fact, at the moment, every inch of her felt wonderful. When she came to the room, she was aware of how many bruises she had acquired from her slip in the stream. But right now, nothing hurt. Not even the wound on her arm. "I think the warm water helps." That, and the way he was touching her, but she didn't have enough nerve to say it.

"Good. I'll ask Cook to prepare you a tea to help ease your muscles. Maybe that will help for later."

Though she nodded again, she became aware of the way he was now rubbing her other foot. Who knew such a simple thing could be so arousing?

His soapy hand traced the length of her other leg, and she noticed the closer he got to the inside of her thigh, the slower he went. At first, she thought it was to further excite her, but there was a cautious expression on his face. He probably wanted to touch her between her legs but wasn't sure he had her permission.

Her heartbeat picking up, she took his hand and brought it to her most secret place. The contact made her tender flesh ache, a curious thing since she couldn't recall ever having such an ache there before. She shifted, hoping he would continue washing her there. And he did, careful as he brushed the bar of soap over her sensitive flesh. She let out a slight moan. She hadn't meant to vocalize her enjoyment of what he was doing, but it slipped out before she could stop it.

"Am I hurting you?" he asked.

She couldn't help but notice that while he directed his question to her, his gaze remained focused on where his hand was. He was leaning in the tub, water sloshing around him, but he didn't seem to notice it. In fact, he didn't seem to be aware of anything but her, and that sent another thrill straight through her.

He finally glanced up at her. "Regina?" he whispered. "Did I hurt you?"

She shook her head. "You didn't hurt me. It felt," her face grew warm, "rather pleasant."

His concerned expression became one of intrigue as he touched her again, this time without the bar of soap hindering him from exploring her with his fingers. His touch was light at first, but before long, he grew bolder, outlining the folds of her flesh, leaving no part of her untended to. She sighed in contentment and leaned back in the tub. Raising her hips to encourage him to continue, she was rewarded for her efforts when he slid a finger into her.

"Is that all right?" he asked.

She murmured that it was and shifted so that he was deeper inside her.

This time he was the one who moaned. "You feel good."

She might have paid more attention to the undeniable trace of arousal in his voice if she hadn't been so preoccupied by the mounting ache between her legs. And as he continued his exploration, she became aware of the parts of her that felt wonderful when he touched them.

Placing her hand over his, she guided his thumb over her sensitive nub and brought another one of his fingers into her. Then she proceeded to join him in his exploration, trying different techniques until she found the one that made her lose all semblance of control.

Her mother would be horrified if she saw her like this, rocking her hips with wild abandon so that water spilled out of the tub. But her mother wasn't here, and since Toby didn't mind it, she gave herself completely to the moment. Once Toby had established the rhythm she liked best, she let go of his hand and gripped the edges of the tub so she could better raise her hips to bring him deeper into her.

He continued stroking her, his fingers teasing the part deep in her while his thumb rubbed her nub. And when she came to the point where she was barely aware of her moans and the way she begged him to keep going, she thought there was no better sensation she'd ever experienced in her entire life. Then before long, she climaxed. Crying out, she stilled and absorbed every part of the moment that she could. She'd never felt anything so incredible. Truly, she had no idea her body was capable of this kind of pleasure. But now that she did, she had every intention of enjoying this again. Many times, in fact.

When the waves of pleasure subsided, her body relaxed, humming with satisfaction. "That was wonderful," she whispered, out of breath.

"Yes, it was," he softly replied then lowered his head so he was kissing the top of her head.

His fingers were still nestled deep inside her, lightly stroking her, something that continued to prolong the lingering effects of her orgasm. She shivered in pleasure and cupped his face in her hands. Lifting her head, she brought his mouth to hers and kissed him. He moaned and deepened the kiss, and soon his tongue was sparring with hers. There was no denying the intensity of his passion. He needed his release, and since he'd given her pleasure, she wanted to do the same for him.

"Take me to the bed," she murmured, wrapping her arms around his neck.

As much as she missed the absence of his fingers when he pulled them out of her, she was eager to make love to him, to find out what it would be like to be filled with him. He carried her to the bed, and after he gently set her down, he removed his wet clothes. She took note of his broad, flat chest with a spattering of dark hair on it. Then her gaze lowered to his hands as he took off his breeches and drawers.

She'd been curious about the part of him that seemed to strain against his breeches when they had shared their passionate embrace at Lord Toplyn's. And now that she got to see that part of him, she found the differences between them fascinating. Maybe she should have been afraid of it, or at least a little intimidated since it was so different from anything she had, but she wasn't. Despite her curiosity, however, she couldn't bring herself to touch it. Not this time anyway. Maybe next time.

Toby joined her on the bed, settling between her legs, and he was soon kissing her again. He didn't enter her right away as she assumed he planned to do since she was very much aware that his penis was pressed against her entrance. But instead, he continued kissing her, the passion in his kisses making the ache between her legs return. She wrapped her legs around his waist and found that when she rubbed intimately against him, it brought back the same pleasure she had experienced in the tub.

With a moan, he reached down between them and guided himself into her. There was a momentary sting as he pressed all the way inside, and he stopped kissing her so he could look at her.

"Should I keep going?" he asked, his voice strained.

She shifted her hips so the discomfort wasn't so noticeable. "Yes," she whispered and moved so that he went deeper into her. She relaxed. That didn't feel bad at all now. "Make love to me, Toby."

Returning his mouth to hers, he did as she wished. Before long, he was moving in and out of her with ease, and she found herself, once again, pulled back into the wonderful place where all she could think about was the pressure building up in her core. Breathless, she ended the kiss and moaned. He murmured her name as he increased the momentum of his thrusting. She reached her peak again, this one not as intense as the one in the tub but just as enjoyable. He stilled and joined her, his body taut, letting out a cry of pleasure as he throbbed inside her, filling her with his seed.

Afterwards, he settled into her arms, his breathing ragged as he kissed her cheek. "Regina," he murmured then kissed her lips. "I love you."

"I love you, too," she softly admitted. She probably loved him from the moment she met him but hadn't realized it until now.

Raising his upper body on his elbows, he studied her face. "Do you?"

A smile tugged at her lips. "I wouldn't have said it if I didn't mean it."

"I wouldn't have either."

"I believe you."

He smiled in return then kissed her again, this one much more gentle, but just as intoxicating. She could get used to this.

Soon, he was cupping her breasts in his hands and teasing her nipples with his tongue in a way that made her want to take him back inside her.

"You keep doing that, and we'll never get out of bed," she warned with a giggle.

He lifted his head and shot her a hopeful smile. "We won't?"

"And the water in the tub will get cold, and we'll have to call up for more hot water."

He glanced back at the tub and snickered. "There's not much water left in there. I'm sure refilling the tub won't be a problem."

"But toweling up all the water on the floor will be."

With a shrug, he brushed her nipple with his thumb, making her shudder in anticipation of what was going to happen next. "I don't mind a little work. I'll clean it up."

"Well, you are responsible for the mess."

He flicked her nipple with his tongue, and she let out a soft groan. "I'm also responsible for messing up the sheets, but something tells me I'll live through it. Besides, I'm not done yet."

As he brought his mouth back to her breast, she sighed. "Good."

And soon he was making love to her again.

Chapter Twenty-Two

Two weeks later, Toby took Regina to the stream, and this time he didn't wear his knit footed drawers, so when he took his boots off, his feet were bare.

"Come on in," Toby encouraged, surprised that she hesitated. "I'll make sure you don't fall in."

"I feel silly," Regina replied as she glanced at the stream.

"You shouldn't. There's no one here but us. I told you, it's a secluded spot."

"Yes," she slowly acknowledged but didn't budge from where she stood.

Amused, he held his hand out to her. "Then why are you waiting? I thought you wanted to do this."

"I do." After a moment, she nodded and picked up her skirt, showing her bare legs, which had healed nicely since she'd taken her tumble. She accepted his hand. "All right. I think I'm ready."

He led her down a small pathway and into the water. The cool water washed over his feet and up past his ankles. She gripped his hand when she almost slipped on a rock. Letting go of her skirt, she wrapped her arms around him, and he chuckled and held her to his side. "I certainly don't mind this."

He kissed the top of her head, and he meant to stop there. But having her in his arms made his mind think of other, more intimate things, and soon he was kissing her cheek and working his way down her neck.

"I'm not sure this is a good place to do this," she murmured, though she didn't sound as if she wanted him to stop.

"I won't let anything bad happen to you," he assured her and pulled her closer.

This time, he brought his mouth to hers. She responded to him, parting her lips as he wished, and he interlaced his tongue with hers. She moaned and leaned into him, just as intent on exploring him as he was in exploring her.

Clasping her hips, he pulled her to him, his arousal pressing nicely against her. She didn't shy away from him but instead seemed to encourage him by snuggling even closer. A low groan escaped his throat as he ran his hands along her body. Even with the layers of clothes she had on, there was no denying how delightful she was.

His lips left hers, and he proceeded to kiss her chin, her cheek, and the skin just below her ear. Her grip tightened on his arms, notifying him that she wanted him just as much as he wanted her. He brought his hands to her breasts and caressed them. He loved how they felt. Soft and full in his hands. She let out another moan. How he loved her. All of her. Her wit, her inner fire, her passion. She was everything a gentleman could want and more. And it was so much better now that she'd completely opened herself to him.

She giggled. "Did you want to go back inside?"

"No," he whispered, out of breath. "I want to show you how much fun it can be to dip your bare feet in cool water on a hot day."

"Seems to me like you'd rather be dipping something else in another place." She wiggled her abdomen against his erection, and he groaned.

"Don't worry. I fully intend to have my way with you later. But," keeping his arm around her waist, he led her down the stream, "right now, I want you to experience the freedom of being out here where there's only you and nature."

"And you."

"Well, yes. That's true." Noting the way she examined her surroundings, he asked, "Didn't you ever do something like this when you were a child?"

"No. My mother would never have approved."

"Hmm." He guided her further down the stream. "I would have thought you were the rebellious sort. You aren't fond of rules, and yet, you seem to follow them."

"As a child, I would have thought this kind of thing unnecessary. Dipping my feet in water outdoors makes no sense when I could do it at home."

"Not everything has to make sense. Sometimes it's all right to do something for the sake of having fun."

"I bet kissing a lady while out here barefoot is more fun than running out here when you were a child."

"That's true. This is a lot more enjoyable. And who knows? Maybe it'll be a romantic place for us," he suggested with a smile.

Returning his smile, she turned her attention to the path in front of them. They stayed there for a good half hour, sometimes stopping to kiss, before they decided to go back to the manor, but only because it was time to change and get ready for dinner.

When they got to the stables, he was surprised to see that Orlando's carriage was nearby.

"Who is it?" she asked him as he helped her down the horse.

"My friend, Orlando," he replied. "He said he'd be by to visit, but I didn't think it'd be so soon. I thought he'd want to stay in London until September."

"Maybe he missed you. I know I would if you were gone."

Pleased, he kissed her despite the fact that the stable boy was right there unsaddling the horses. "I'm glad you'd miss me."

"And what about you?" she asked, her eyes twinkling. "Would you miss me?"

"Terribly."

Her smile widened, and he took her by the arm and led her to the manor. As they neared the front door, he saw Orlando wave through the window of the drawing room. With a grin, he returned the gesture and told her, "There he is."

She glanced at the window. "I don't think I said much more to him than a couple words in the past."

"Good. He happens to be a likable fellow. I'd hate for you to have fallen in love with him instead of me."

She giggled as they walked up the steps.

As soon as the footman opened the door, Orlando entered the entryway. "I was beginning to think you fell into that stream you like to go to."

Toby caught the way Regina raised her eyebrow and said, "He used to go down there with me when we were children."

"Yes, and here I thought being a married gentleman would make you put away childish things," Orlando joked.

"I don't recall there being a rule that says gentlemen can't take off their boots and enjoy a relaxing walk in the stream." Since Regina's cheeks grew pink, he decided to change the conversation. Most likely, she didn't want anyone to know she'd joined him in that walk because she didn't want them to know she'd taken off her stockings outdoors. "Regina, I believe you remember Orlando from our wedding."

"It's a pleasure to meet you again, my lord," she said with a curtsy.

"And it's a pleasure to see you again as well, my lady," Orlando said with a bow.

"I hope you don't mind if I change for dinner," she said, glancing at Toby.

"Go on ahead. I'll change in a little while."

With a nod, she told Orlando she'd talk to him later and headed for the stairs.

Toby turned to Orlando and gestured to the drawing room. "How long have you been here?"

"About forty-five minutes."

Toby saw the butler had already brought him tea and scones. "I'm sorry you waited for such a long time. Had I any idea you were coming so soon, I would have been here." He sat down and poured himself and Orlando a cup of tea.

"To be fair, I didn't give you any warning. I hadn't intended to stop by so soon, but since I was on my way to my estate, I thought I'd come by and see how things are going. You know, with you and Regina."

"I didn't realize you worried about us."

"I wouldn't say 'worried'. It was more of a concern." He sat in the other chair and accepted the cup of tea. "You're my friend. Of course, I wondered how you were doing. I thought I'd offer my assistance if needed. You know, assure her that things weren't the way Pennella was trying to make them seem. But from what I saw, you two have already worked through everything."

"Yes, we have. She's a very forgiving lady."

"I'm glad to hear it."

Toby drank his tea and glanced at his friend. "How long will you stay?"

"I won't be more than two days. I don't want to intrude on a couple in love."

Toby grinned. "I had no idea love could feel so wonderful."

"I can tell. You never smiled that way around me. I must say I'm hurt. I thought our friendship meant something."

Laughing, Toby put his cup down and motioned for him to stand up. "I'll show you to your room. You'll be happy to see everything has finally been dusted."

"What a relief. I don't want to wake up covered in cobwebs again."

"No, you don't," Toby replied, playing along. "Last time you were here, it took me a whole three days before I found you. At first, I thought you were a great big caterpillar trapped in a cocoon."

"Thank goodness I don't have to worry about that this time."

With another chuckle, Toby showed him to his room.

WHEN REGINA FINISHED getting ready for dinner, she went to the drawing room and was surprised to see Orlando sitting alone with a book. "Good evening, Orlando," she said as he glanced up at her. "I thought Toby would be down here already."

"I'm afraid not. They say ladies take forever to get ready, but honestly, I'd say he's worse."

She chuckled at his joke and sat on the settee. Since Orlando was Toby's friend, she thought it was only fair to spend time with him and get to know him. Toby spoke so highly of him that she figured he was the kind of person who'd make a good friend. "I hope you had a pleasant trip out here."

"I did." He set the book aside and added, "I only plan to be here for two days. I'm on my way to my estate. It's about half a day from here."

"Oh, you don't have to leave on my account. You and Toby have been friends for a long time. You should play chess or talk or do whatever else it is gentlemen do."

"I appreciate the offer, but I think he'd rather spend his time with you."

Her face warmed with pleasure at his words. And to think when she left London, she had been afraid of what being alone here with Toby would mean. But now she found she'd be very happy if they never went to London again. Well, except perhaps to see her parents. That was the only thing that could lure her back.

She cleared her throat and smiled at him. "Toby said that you two have known each other since childhood."

"Our parents were friends who'd get together from time to time. I believe we were actually babies when we first met."

"That long ago?"

"To be fair, I don't remember the actual event, but I remember my mother saying I could stink up a room. No need to fear, my lady. I have since learned to avoid such embarrassing mishaps."

She laughed. "I can see why Toby likes you. You have a marvelous sense of humor."

"I try to see the best in things."

"I'd say you succeed very well."

After a moment of silence passed between them, he asked, "So is everything all right between you and my friend?"

She didn't catch his meaning right away, but when she did, she nodded. "Yes. It's not like it was when we married."

"Good. One of the reasons I came by was to assure you that despite that wager my friend made with Pennella, he really did love you."

"Did he?" She had hoped that was the case, but it was nice to hear.

"He did. Not that he planned to when he picked you. His original plan was to protect you from Pennella and quietly let you out of the engagement. But before long, he realized he wanted to marry you. I just wanted you to know it wasn't as heartless as it seemed."

"Thank you, Orlando." Even if she had overcome most of her doubts about the wager, this helped to resolve all of them once and for all. "Toby's fortunate to have such a good friend."

"You know, I tell him that all the time, and he doesn't believe me."

She laughed at his joke then noticed a movement out of the corner of her eye. She glanced at the doorway and saw Toby.

"I'm sorry I kept you waiting," Toby said.

"Don't be." She waved him over to sit by her. "It gave me a chance to get to know your friend under better conditions."

Toby settled next to her and clasped his hand around hers. "I hope he didn't tell you nonsense like waking up covered in cobwebs last time he stayed here."

Her eyes wide, she looked at Orlando. "Did that really happen?"

Orlando laughed. "No, but I was afraid it would happen. Fortunately, this place is in much better shape than it used to be."

"It wasn't as bad as I thought it'd be when he warned me about it," she told Orlando.

The butler came into the room and announced that dinner was ready. Accepting Toby's arm, she rose to her feet and joined the gentlemen as they left the room.

Chapter Twenty-Three

The next afternoon, Toby glanced up from the book he was reading in the drawing room while Orlando taught Regina how to play chess. Though he played the game from time to time, he had no interest in playing it enough to teach it to her. But since she had expressed the desire to learn it, he couldn't say no when Orlando offered to show her what to do. And that had been all fine and good until Toby realized she was laughing at all the amusing stories Orlando insisted on telling her. If Toby had known his friend was going to be so charming, he would have taught her the boring thing himself.

"I don't believe that at all," she said, laughing while she moved her pawn forward.

"I might have exaggerated just a little," Orlando consented. "Toby did scream and run into the drawing room. But in all fairness, he did think the snake was a common adder."

Toby grimaced. "Must you tell her that story?"

"She's already seen your birthmark," Orlando replied and shrugged.

"Yes, and thanks to you for slipping a snake into my tub, everyone else who happened to be here that day knows about it, too."

"You were only eight. No one can fault you for rushing out of your room without covering up first. Now," Orlando moved his bishop diagonally on the board, "if you were to do that today, it'd be something to really talk about."

She chuckled then glanced at Toby and cleared her throat. "You must not tell such stories, Orlando. It's not nice. Toby hasn't told me your most embarrassing moments, so it's not fair you do that to him."

"He should tell you. There are some good ones." Orlando winked at Toby. "Do you want to tell her about the time I greeted Lady Westfell by the wrong title?"

Her eyebrows rose in interest, but Toby shook his head. "Not really." He turned his attention back to the book. "You do it."

"What title did you call her?" she asked Orlando.

"Lady Wasteful. It was an error. I was nervous."

"Well, she was wasteful," Toby added. "She never wore the same clothes twice, would ask for a large plate of food and only eat a couple bites, and..." When he realized Orlando was telling Regina to move the knight over two squares instead of one, he stopped talking.

"Now, move it up or down," Orlando said once she moved it over another square.

She moved the knight down and nodded. Then she looked over at Toby. "What were you saying about Lady Westfell?"

"Nothing," he finally said after a quick debate over whether or not he should make the effort to repeat himself. What did it matter? Between the two of them, Orlando always had a better way of telling a story.

He turned his attention back to the book but read very little of it. As much as he tried not to let their constant chatter about everything but chess bother him, the longer the game went, the harder it was for him to sit still. He knew Orlando would never sleep with her, and he didn't think she was the type who'd take a lover. But he couldn't help but wonder if she secretly wished she had married Orlando instead of him. Orlando wasn't deceitful like Pennella, but he was definitely charming.

When they finally decided they'd had enough of chess, it was time to change for dinner, and he sighed with relief and escorted her to her bedchamber.

DURING DINNER, REGINA kept glancing at Toby. What was wrong with him? He'd been relaxed the previous evening while they ate. He'd even been talkative that morning. But at some point in the afternoon, he'd become withdrawn, and for the life of her, she couldn't figure out why. Surely, he'd be happy to have his friend here. But the longer into the day they got, the less he engaged in the conversation. She felt it was up to her to respond to Orlando just so he had someone to talk to.

She finally realized what was bothering Toby when she laughed at one of the amusing stories Orlando told her. In her desire to get along with Toby's friend, she must have unintentionally done or said something that made Toby worry she'd rather be married to Orlando than him.

When dinner was over, she thanked both gentlemen for a lovely evening and feigned a headache so she could let them spend the rest of their evening without her. In light of everything, she sensed it was her best recourse. She retired to her bedchamber and let her lady's maid get her ready for bed.

But instead of going to sleep, she curled up on her settee by the window and read a book she'd been meaning to get to for a while. Just as she reached the fifth chapter, she heard a movement from Toby's bedchamber and knew he had retired for the evening. She waited until she heard his valet leave before she knocked on the door adjoining their rooms.

He opened the door, his eyes wide. "I thought you'd be asleep."

"No, I just thought it best if I come up here early and read." She motioned to his room. "Mind if I come in?"

"Of course not." He stepped aside to let her in. He shut the door and turned to her. "Do you feel better?"

"I feel fine. I didn't have a headache."

"Then why did you say you had one?"

She clasped her hands in front of her and smiled at him. "Because I thought it best, given the circumstances."

"The circumstances?"

"Toby, I want to apologize for spending so much time with Orlando."

He let out an uneasy chuckle and headed over to the table. "Orlando's our guest. You were only being polite."

"Yes. But he's also your friend, and I wanted to get to know him because of that. So in the future," she continued as he lit the candles, "we'd both get to welcome him as our friend."

"That's understandable."

"In my eagerness to get along with him, I might have overdone it."

He glanced at her. "Orlando's always been good with people. He makes them feel comfortable. It's only natural you liked him."

With a sigh, she watched as he went to the window and started pulling the drapes together. "I do like him, and I'm glad I like him because he's your friend. But," she went over to him and placed her hand on his arm, "I love you."

HER MEANING TOOK A moment to sink in, and when it did, Toby suddenly felt foolish for thinking she had wished she'd married Orlando instead of him. Because he could see she didn't. She loved him. And only him.

Relieved, he took her into his arms and kissed her. She slid her arms under his and leaned into him, her breasts pressing against his chest. Since she was wearing her nightclothes, it afforded a much better feel of her body. He ran his hands down her back and cupped her behind in his hands. She wiggled against him, her abdomen rubbing intimately against his erection. Having not made love to her earlier that day, the kiss made him that much more eager to be with her. Letting go of her, he removed their clothes so there would be nothing else separating them. He took a moment to gaze at her body in the candlelight, noting the way her breath quickened and her skin flushed at his perusal.

"I like it when you don't have anything on," he whispered then drew her back into his arms and brought his lips to hers.

She moaned and deepened the kiss, her tongue tracing his lower lip until he received her into his mouth. She was no longer shy about showing her desire for him, something he was grateful for as she lowered her hands. He lightly squeezed her arms, encouraging her to touch him intimately so he could feel those wonderful hands around his male hardness that grew thicker in anticipation.

One hand wrapped around his erection while the other cupped his testicles, lightly massaging them. She'd quickly become an expert in learning how to stroke him, starting at the base of his shaft and bringing her hand up in a swift motion that made him groan in pleasure. Oh, she was wonderful. So very wonderful. How did he ever get fortunate enough to marry a lady who possessed so much passion beneath the surface? She continued her ministrations, and he murmured his appreciation, his hips moving slightly as she established a rhythm that could very easily make him climax.

"Regina," he whispered against her mouth then brushed his tongue over hers.

Ending the kiss, he opened his eyes so he could focus on the candelabra in the room, something that effectively simmered his blood enough so he could delay the inevitable.

She released him then knelt in front of him. Curious, he watched, both in awe and anticipation, as she took him into her mouth. Several times, she twirled her tongue around his tip, starting at its ridge and moving to the slit, an action that made him shiver in pleasure. He gulped and massaged her shoulders, whispering her name and gently rocking his hips so that he could move in and out of her mouth, careful not to go too far in.

Soon. Soon, he'd be fully inside her body, and he'd plunge deep inside her then. For now, he was content to slide gently in and out of her, and she held him at the base of his shaft to better angle him, heightening the sensation. He let out a groan and focused once more on the candelabra, willing the urge to climax to subside. But every nerve in his body screamed for release, and he knew if he didn't stop right now, he would lose control.

"Regina," he rasped and pulled out of her.

His penis protested, but he helped her to her feet. His gaze met hers and he kissed her, his hands going to her breasts and lightly squeezing them. She responded to him, her kisses as anxious as his, signaling her mounting desire. He carried her to the edge of the bed and encouraged her to lie down in front of him. He spread her legs and took note of the wonderful view of her pink flesh, which welcomed him to enter her. He traced her moist flesh and groaned, delighted that she was so wet he could slide easily into her.

He scooted her toward him then entered her. She let out a contented sigh, and he shifted so he was deeper in her core. He slid almost all the way out of her then back in, using the same slow and controlled movements he'd used when he'd been in her mouth. She groaned and gripped the back of his thighs, pulling him fully into her.

"Eager for me, are you?" he whispered, excited by the way she started rocking her hips, her expression a mixture of pleasure and pain.

He leaned forward and cupped one breast in his hand while he brought his other hand between them and fondled her sensitive nub. She moaned, louder this time, and her flesh squeezed around him. He focused on her face, wanting to watch her as she worked toward her peak, delighting in how he could make her lose control to the point where she started crying out his name, letting him know she was thinking of him during their lovemaking.

She felt like heaven around him, her flesh pulling him deeper into her, and when she cried out in pleasure, he lost what little control he had. He gritted his teeth and shuddered above her, releasing his seed and joining her at the heights of ecstasy. He had wanted to prolong the moment, to give her another orgasm before he finally came, but everything felt much too good. And it wasn't like this would be their only time making love. He'd make sure she received her pleasure again before the night was over. All they'd done just now was get warmed up.

Gasping, he collapsed in her arms and embraced her. "I don't know how it's possible," he rasped, "but our time together only gets better."

She murmured her agreement.

After his head cleared, he spent considerable time kissing her, savoring the moment, assured that she truly wanted to be with him—and only him. "Regina?" he whispered.

"Hmm?"

"Thank you for making my life perfect."

Looking up at him, she cupped the back of his neck and brought his mouth back to hers for another kiss. And before long, they were making love again.

"I HOPE YOU'LL MAKE it by here again before next year," Toby told Orlando the next morning as he stood in the entryway to say good-bye to his friend.

"You can always visit me," Orlando replied. "I have more than enough room for you and your wife, and," he added as Regina came over to them, "I need to see if she won that last game of chess because she's good at it or because she just got lucky."

Toby slipped his arm around her waist and grinned. "I don't know. I have a feeling she's smarter than you."

"Oh, Toby." She shook her head, but her smile betrayed how flattered she was that he chose to compliment her.

"I don't care much for the game myself," he admitted. "I suppose having you around will finally give him someone to play it with, and he prefers a challenge so don't go easy on him."

"I won't," she promised. "It was a pleasure to get to know you better, Orlando."

"It's good to see that my friend is happy," Orlando told her then shot Toby a pointed look. "Maybe now you'll smile when you go to London."

"I smiled." He glanced at her, noting her raised eyebrows. "I smiled. Often. I was always a happy gentleman."

"I amend what I said," Orlando consented. "He's been happy ever since I came into his life. Before that, all he did was cry."

"We were infants."

"It wasn't so long after meeting me that you spoke your first word. To my dying day, I'll swear it was 'Orlando.'"

"I'm not sure anyone's first word can be 'Orlando,'" Regina replied.

"It might have been more like an 'O', but I know what he meant." Orlando winked.

"Get on to your estate," Toby said and shooed him out the open door. "Don't keep your coachman waiting."

Orlando glanced at his carriage then tipped his hat to them. "Until we meet again, my lady, keep Toby out of trouble."

"I will," she called out as he bounded down the steps.

"Trouble?" Toby asked, turning back to her as the footman shut the door.

"Well, you have been known to get into quite a bit of trouble in the past," she replied as she headed for the drawing room.

She glanced over her shoulder, and her expression indicated that she wanted him to follow her. And as she wished, he obeyed. When he stepped into the room, she shut the doors and turned back to him, her hands behind her back.

His gaze went to the doors then back to her. "Why do I have the nagging suspicion this isn't going to be in my favor?"

"Oh, it could be in your favor," she said as she stepped over to him, just stopping shy of her breasts touching his chest.

He arched an eyebrow. "It sounds promising, but I sense you're up to something."

"Well, it's true. I do have something in mind."

"And that would be...?"

A mischievous smile lit up her face and her green eyes twinkled. "A wager. With me."

"I don't know. I've had enough of wagers to last me a lifetime."

"Aren't you even interested in what it's about?"

"Not really."

She wrapped her arms around his neck and snuggled up to him. "How about now?"

Bringing his hands to her waist, he said, "I could be convinced as long as the terms are favorable."

She stroked the back of his neck. "They are. It's something I know you'll enjoy."

"All right. What do you want to wager?"

"I bet you that I can make it to the stream before you do."

Not sure he heard her right since he had expected her to suggest something of a sexual nature, he asked, "What?"

"We don't start for the stream until we're both on the horses. You can run faster than me, and that's an unfair advantage. I want this to be something I have an equal chance of winning."

"You want to race horses to the stream?"

She nodded and released him. "Yes. I thought it'd be fun to go there again. We'll take off our boots and go for a walk."

"Go for a walk?"

She went over to the drawing room doors.

"But I thought..." He glanced at the settee, the chair, the desk, the wall... All possible places they could make love. "I thought you had something more intimate in mind."

She opened the doors and looked at him, her eyes wide. "My lord, just what kind of lady do you take me for?" When he didn't respond, she added, "Oh, I forgot to add the last part."

"What's that?"

She gestured for him to come over to her, and though he wasn't sure he'd be any more eager to hear it than he was to hear this wager was a simple race to the stream, he did as she bid. Standing on her tiptoes, she whispered in his ear, "The loser has to pleasure the winner in whatever way the winner prefers." She settled back on her feet, a wicked gleam in her eye. "Care to make a wager?"

A smile tugged at his lips. "All right. You got yourself a wager."

Giggling, she hurried out the front door, and he followed.

Epilogue

June 1816

Regina watched as her mother fluttered about the drawing room, sorting through an assortment of different colors. "Mother, keep in mind that the baby will either be a girl or a boy. You should pick colors that go with both."

"I know, but pink is so pretty." Her mother turned to the seamstress. "I can have a pink gown made, and if it turns out to be a boy, we'll just save it for the next baby. Surely, Regina can manage one girl in the number of children she'll have."

Regina rolled her eyes but smiled as she rubbed her belly. How she looked forward to giving birth next month so this nonsense over colors would stop. "I can't guarantee a girl or a boy. The baby will be whatever it will be."

"I'm partial to girls. You can go shopping with a granddaughter. You can decorate her hair and put her in the loveliest of gowns. You can even help her secure a titled gentleman when she comes of age. But a boy? What can a grandmother do with a boy?"

"You can take him horseback riding, take him to the circus, show him a hot air balloon... You can even instruct him on what he can do to secure a lady who comes from a good background."

"I suppose you're right," her mother agreed. "But I do so love shopping and pretty dresses."

Regina glanced at the seamstress. "We'll have clothing made for a boy and a girl. That way, whichever one we have, we're prepared."

The baby in her womb kicked, and Regina took that as her little one's agreement.

The seamstress nodded and waited as her mother selected the shades of the various colors she wanted. As the seamstress gathered her materials and left, the butler came in to announce Lady Seyton's arrival.

Regina's eyebrows rose. "Lady Seyton isn't here to give lessons to my child already, is she?" she asked her mother.

"Of course not," her mother replied. "Just what kind of lady do you take me for? I wouldn't begin my granddaughter's lessons until she learns to walk."

Despite Regina's groan, she couldn't help but chuckle. For her mother's sake, she hoped she had a girl. The poor woman would be at her wit's end waiting for the next baby to be born.

When Helena entered the room, Regina began to stand up from the settee, but Helena motioned for her to stay seated. "There's no need for formalities," Helena said. She turned to Regina's mother. "You wished to speak with me?"

"Yes." Her mother encouraged Helena to sit next to Regina then sat in the chair nearby. "I'd like to know what names gentlemen find most attractive."

"Oh, you can't be serious, Mother," Regina argued.

"She's not here to give my granddaughter lessons," her mother replied, looking shocked Regina would even object. "I merely want to pick a good name for her."

"Toby and I already have names picked out."

"Yes, but we need to make sure they're good ones. A lady's name is one of her most important assets. Why, I thought long and hard before I decided on Regina."

Helena chuckled. "And a fine name it is, too. It sounds like a lady who's intelligent and beautiful."

"See?" her mother told Regina. "And that is exactly what you are, dear. I want my granddaughter to receive a similar blessing. Never underestimate the power of a good name."

"But this might be a boy." Regina glanced at Helena. "Can you believe what I have to go through?" She spent all winter looking forward to seeing her mother again, and now all she wanted to do was head right back to Greenwood.

"But if my granddaughter is a girl, it doesn't hurt to be prepared, and who better than Helena to offer advice?"

Helena placed a comforting hand on Regina's arm. "Actually," she directed her gaze to her mother, "I have extended my services to helping gentlemen secure a worthy lady by the end of the Season, so if you have a grandson, I can help him as well."

"I didn't realize you were offering lessons to gentlemen," Regina said, surprised.

"I only started this a couple days ago," Helena said.

"What convinced you to do it?"

"A duke came to me and said he needs a wife before the end of the month. I wasn't going to agree, but it's apparent he doesn't know the first thing about ladies." She shrugged. "I figured, why not? Whether I'm helping ladies or gentlemen, the basic rules still apply, except gentlemen need to think more with their heads when trying to find a wife."

"Well, this is wonderful. Then we can discuss names for girls and boys." Her mother clapped her hands together. "I was thinking Angelica for a girl. Or perhaps Eloise. Of course, there's always Clementina. If the child must be a boy, then I think Reginal will suit."

Regina gagged. "Mother, I will not name a boy Reginal. I don't care how much you wish it."

Thankfully, the front door to her parents' townhouse opened, and she heard her father and Toby talking. She would have jumped up if she could have managed the feat, but the baby's weight made it impossible, so she settled for standing up in a more ladylike fashion. That was just as well since her mother would have been appalled if she had, indeed, jumped.

"Good luck with teaching the duke what he needs to know to secure a wife," Regina told Helena. Turning to her mother, she added, "Toby and I have already decided on Judith if the baby's a girl, but you may think over other possible boy names." She headed for Toby and her father then stopped and looked back at her mother. "I mean it, Mother. No Reginal."

Her mother sighed but consented to her wishes.

"How are you feeling, Regina?" Toby asked as she came into the entryway.

"Fine, though Mother is being her usual self," she replied then smiled at her father.

"You can't blame her," her father replied. "She's excited about the grandchild."

"Excited isn't the word. I'd say she's obsessed."

He chuckled. "She means well."

"I know, but she's determined the child will be a girl. For her sake, I hope she's right. I don't want to go through another nine months of this," she said.

"Hopefully, you won't have to." Toby kissed her. "Are you ready to go to Hyde Park?"

She nodded and said good-bye to her father, glad to get a reprieve from her mother. As much as she loved her, she could only take so much.

She slipped her arm around Toby's. "I'm glad to see you."

"Because I saved you from your mother?" he teased as he led her down the townhouse steps.

"No, though you make a good point." She chuckled. "But what I meant was, I missed you."

"I missed you, too. There's no one else I'd rather share the day with than you."

Her gaze met his, and he smiled at her. Returning his smile, she squeezed his arm. Then, together, they headed for Hyde Park, content to enjoy the rest of their day.

Don’t miss the other books in the Marriage by Deceit Series!

Love Lessons With The Duke: Book 2

THE DUKE OF ASHBOURNE asks Lady Seyton to help him secure a bride in one month, but soon he realizes he's in love with her and will do anything it takes to marry her, even if it involves a scandal.

Ruined by the Earl: Book 3

After losing all of his money in a reckless bet, Logan Breckman, the Earl of Toplyn, needs to marry a lady from a wealthy family–and fast. So he does the only thing he can think of and picks one at random to trick into marriage.

The Earl's Stolen Bride: Book 4

Orlando Emmett, the Earl of Reddington, fell in love with Chloe as soon as he met her. Unfortunately, she married Lord Hawkins before he could propose. Now, a year later, she's a widow. And while he should honor the mourning period, he's afraid if he doesn't act fast, he might not get another chance to be her husband. So he plans a way to make sure he gets her before someone else does.

Also by Ruth Ann Nordin

Husbands for the Larson Sisters Series
Suitable for Marriage
Daisy's Prince Charming

Marriage by Deceit Series
The Earl's Secret Bargain
Love Lessons With the Duke
Ruined by the Earl
The Earl's Stolen Bride

Marriage by Design Series
Breaking the Rules
Nobody's Fool

Marriage by Necessity Series
A Perilous Marriage
The Cursed Earl

Marriage by Obligation Series
Secret Admirer

Marriage by Scandal Series
The Earl's Inconvenient Wife

Nebraska Prairie Series
Interview for a Wife

Pioneer Series
The Marriage Agreement

Wyoming Series
The Outlaw's Bride
The Rancher's Bride
The Fugitive's Bride
The Loner's Bride

Standalone
The Duke's Secluded Bride
A Deceptive Wager
An Earl In Time
Her Counterfeit Husband

Watch for more at https://ruthannnordinauthorblog.com/.

About the Author

Ruth Ann Nordin has written over 100 books, most of them being Regencies and historical western romances. As fun as writing is, she has also learned that time with family and friends is just as important. She has also learned that writing for passion is the best reason to write since it is what sustains an author's work for the long haul. That's why she's been able to keep writing for as long as she had. It's hard to believe she started out in ebooks back in 2009. How time flies.

Read more at https://ruthannnordinauthorblog.com/.

Ingram Content Group UK Ltd.
Milton Keynes UK
UKHW021130180423
420361UK00015B/1086